I have worked with young peop
backgrounds for 20 years. I am a youth worker and have
several professional qualifications in the youth work and
health and social care sector. I have worked in the child
care system for the local authority, private and for a
charity. In the past 12 years I have worked specifically
with young people who have been in alternative
provision academies, in care, in prisons and Young
Offenders Institutions as well as young homeless people
on the streets.

Stories of 'spice zombies' have become an all too common national headline, with Manchester often at the forefront of media coverage. Set in Manchester's young homeless community, *The Spice Boys* provides a unique insight into the life of the increasing number of young homeless people who populate the UK's city centres. Drawing on privileged access and many years of first-hand experience of working with vulnerable young people, the author shines a light on the dark and often unseen reality of street homelessness. The impact of synthetic cannabinoids more commonly known as 'Spice' on this community is artfully crafted and true to reality. These often harsh realities are laid bear with no punches pulled yet humour and hope accompany the heartache, making this a captivating read.

Dr Rob Ralphs, *Reader in Criminology, Manchester Metropolitan University*

Based on Peter Morgan's true life experiences as a support worker, *The Spice Boys* grabs a joint in one hand and leads us through the mean streets of Manchester by the other. This book is as eye-opening as it is engaging and shines a much-needed spotlight on the issues that young homeless people face today. *The Spice Boys* is a comprehensive introduction to the darkest dimensions of the UK's drug laws, which punish rather than protect the most vulnerable members of our population.

Rosalind Stone, *Features Writer, VolteFace*

Dedication

The book is dedicated to all the staff and volunteers who work on the front line with Looked After Children and in the homeless sector. I would like to thank Cheryl, my mum, Tink and Paula for your support, encouragement and belief in me.

#endyouthhomelessness
#homelessnesshasnoplace

Peter Morgan

THE SPICE BOYS

AUSTIN MACAULEY PUBLISHERS™

LONDON • CAMBRIDGE • NEW YORK • SHARJAH

A CIP catalogue record for this title is available from the British Library.

ISBN 978-1-78710-556-0 (Paperback)
ISBN 978-1-78710-557-7 (E-Book)

www.austinmacauley.com

First Published (2017)
Austin Macauley Publishers Ltd.™
25 Canada Square
Canary Wharf
London
E14 5LQ

The Spice Boys is about four young people from Manchester who are homeless and addicted to SPICE a "Legal High" which has plagued the city for several years.

The Spice Boys will give you an in-depth reality of the hardships, politics and truths of modern day homelessness and how society manages with young people who have been in the care system, prison system and homelessness.

The story revolves around Ricky, Mo, George and Vinnie. The twelve month journey will take you to some of the darkest cruellest places life has to offer via the childcare system to prison and back onto the streets! However, as with everything in life, some humour always eases the reality!

All characters are fictional, however the stories and events may have actually happened to numerous people's lives who have come through the young people's support foundation, youth hostels, childcare homes, prison, young offenders institutions and of course… those who end up on the street.

Part 1

1

Dark January

George

Monday January 19th. I'm on my way to court for my sentencing. Obviously I went guilty because I could not be arsed waiting for the duty solicitor on Monday and I did it anyway. Obviously we are not gonna let the security guard in Tesco Express spit in my boy's face. If he would have just let us take the crate of beers then all this wouldn't have happened. I did not actually throw the sign through the glass door when they barricaded themselves in; in fact I was just there.

The CCTV in court does not show the security guard spitting in Mikey's face, but it does show him butting the security guard. I'm not saying Mikey was lying but obviously if he did then we was right to give it him.

When I get there my support worker is there, obviously Amy my leaving care worker has told him I would be here today. I'm looking at six months do three, but I have already done four weeks so I will be out soon and I have got burn and spice in me now. On the last visit Lee was really going on at me for minding the phones inside me and the gear, but I get sorted for it so I am not arsed. Sometimes you can feel them actually moving up your stomach but I know how to do it all now so I am not arsed.

Court's been dragging out all day and I just want to be sentenced to the six months and get back but then the barrister gets Lee to speak on my behalf for me. He goes pure white when he realises he has to swear on the Bible. Talk about a fucking duck out of water.

Lee begins to mitigate on Georges behalf.

"George has had a completely traumatic life; he has no concept of home. I believe he is suffering from post-traumatic stress disorder from when he was raped when he was living in a care home."

Officially, George was not raped, as the offender (who was another young person in care) was found not guilty on the charge against George but he was actually convicted of the two other rape charges on the other boys.

"I believe that the anxiety he lives with means he cannot settle in any place. We are doing our all to get him accommodated in a home or house which is run by two people that have being fostering and supporting homeless people from a "family home" type manor for many years. He needs this full-on support to get him back into life and society. The situation we are stuck with is that we cannot refer him to the golden house until he is released from prison. As he is a care leaver, the local authority has to accommodate him until he is twenty-one. If he was released today I could speak with his Barnardo's worker who will put him into a B&B

tonight and I will speak with the housing team at YPSF (Young People's Support Foundation) and have him accommodated as soon as possible at a supported accommodation until we can get a placement in the golden house. My only concern is him engaging with the programme, I have faith he will." Judge Brown –"you have to as it is your work" Lee quickly responds in agreement –"yes your honour."

The judge obviously is not arsed about me, anyway he sentences Mikey to nine months and he is taken down... I am given a six month suspended sentence which I am buzzing about. I have to go see Lee and go to Barnardo's tonight and my conditions are to engage with the programme and I have to go back on the 18th of February and if I've not been doing what I agreed to on the programme he will slam me to the six month... I'm not arsed anyway.

2

Elysium

Ricky

I see some lads ahead I know from when I used to do the street robberies as I get to the shop on Bury New Road. Elysium sells spice and is open early and closes late which is good for me as I need to be close to the shop at all times. If I have not got anything I will wait for ten minutes and someone with money who I know will be going in. I see Preston who is in a bad way. He is on that homemade "annihilation 44" made by the guys in the shop. They use Japanese knotweed dried up, crushed then they spray the drug on it. Ever since Preston's been on that his head has well gone. The dirty fucker's even begging in the gardens now! I will never go down on that floor for money, ever. The lads are mugging Preston for his bag again; it's his own fucking fault. I told him loads of times I will sell to him so he does not get taxed down here... some people will just not listen, but like I say you can't help everyone.

"Aright Ricky," says Dermo.

In the papers he was said to be from one of the most feared family in Salford, but I have always got on well with him. I had to stab one of his mates a few years ago for taking the piss, we had a run in about it and since then he has been fine, but thinking about it, lately I've noticed he's started speaking to me like the homeless scruffs who beg like Preston. I AM NOT LIKE THESE FUCKERS I AM NEVER GONNA BE LIKE THEM ONCE THE SPICE IS BANNED I AM GETTING OFF IT.

"Alright Dermo, what's been happening Bro?"

Dermo goes on about the birds he's banging and other shit, I don't really want to engage "ENGAGE"? I sound like them support worker fuckers from the YPSF … I don't really want to chat shit! I want to get my gear and go. The cheeky fucker tries to sell me some smack before I go in the shop as well, I suppose it could be better for me at the minute as the lads in prison found it easier to get off heroin than they did spice!! It's madness. But fuck them I need to get off and skin up.

3

Wigan Social Services

Mo

The police drop me back at the care home at 01.30. I have been missing from home for thirteen days and I will be going back to the homeless camps tomorrow as soon as I have had a kip, shower and something to eat. I am not staying here. Fuck that. I know most of the staff don't give a fuck when I go anyway as it just makes there twenty-four hour shift easier as there are only three in the house rather than four of us. I hate these here too, not the staff, the others that live here; they don't understand.

I go down for breakfast after my shower and have fresh clothes on. Claire is on shift and wants to talk to me about where I have been and informs me I have missed all my appointments. I just had half a joint of spice in my room so I really cannot fully understand what she's saying I just want some food my spends which is 2 weeks THEY'VE GOT TO GIVE IT ME and then I am off back to Manchester...

I have my breakfast and listen to Jade and Matthew fighting in the living room over a cig. For once Matthew gets the better of her and gives her a black eye but she's bit his arm and it looks like she really hurt him this time. This probably means they are not going into school now and that means the staff will have a mad house all day, not that I will be here to see it like.

Claire puts a letter on the table in front of me …

Mohammed Khan
22 Winters Road
Wigan
WN 2 1YY
PAYMENT of £60 Manchester Metrolink service

Dear Mr Khan

On the 02/01/15 you were travelling on the Manchester to Altrincham Metro line with no valid ticket to use the service.

Please make payment to the attached document within 30 days of receiving this letter. Should you have not paid within this time you will be given a court summons to appear at Manchester Magistrates Court which may result in you paying £100.00 fine plus court charges.

Yours sincerely
D. Holmes
MML Passenger Relations Manager

I have another one to come from the other night as well but they can pay it I'm not. I will go to Forrest Bank nick before I pay that fine. I ask Claire for my spends and she says that I have to pay my metro fine!

We argue for about ten minutes until I hear Dave in the office saying that we HAVE to give him 50% of his spends and cannot deduct any more as they would be breaking the law and breeching my human rights. This is good news I did not know this. I will not tell them idiots I live with but save this for ammo when I need back up or to stir some shit up in the house. I hear them talking about me being high and vulnerable at the camps and having concerns about me not taking my prescribed medication and trying to take my own life again and something about being solicited. God knows what that is… I think I DO know what it is. I can look after myself and we are all right down there together; it will be even better when George gets out. I then go out of the house leaving the door open to stop them realising I have gone.

4

My Dad's Gaff

Vinnie

I can't fucking stay here with him any longer, I am going to fucking crack up or do something even worse to HIM! If my daughters saw me and I was like him I would top myself, rather than be a piss head on fucking White Lightning, bladdered every morning and night; he's a fucking disgrace.

I have to be out early as the housing team and support workers come round early to check on him and see if I have been here. Apparently I am abusing him and causing him physical harm. Bollocks; we had one fight and it was his fucking fault for talking about my mam like he did and I am not allowed to stay here I am sick of having to do a runner every time the door goes and most of the time it's fucking Lee checking on me. I don't need his help, but the bus passes and McDonalds do come in handy. Speaking of which, I wonder if they can get me a gym pass. I will get on to that once he puts some credit on the phone he got me.

"Dad I'm going, I might be back later on tonight why don't you go and get in the bed now."

"What time is it Vinnie? Is the offy open yet?" Moans Vinnie Snr.

"Yeah it is but I have to get off, I have took a couple of cigs, see ya later."

5

On The Outside

George

They let me out at seven o'clock, I was released at four fifteen I was banging fuck out of the door. They told me that they sent the fax to Strangeways who did not return the release documents until six forty-five. Strangeways Prison is one mile away from the court house steps. I could've walked there and back in thirty mins; piss takers the lot of 'em.

When I get out to reception Lee is not there, but he has left a tenner with the security and a note saying ring Amy, she will book me a B&B for the night and we can go to the town hall tomorrow and get me accommodated. The thing is, Matty and his girl Jo are waiting for me. Matty has gone not guilty and will be tried next month. They tell me the same shit that Lee has said to them, but obviously I am not going to ring Amy now. I go to stay at Matty's mam's for the night and I'll sort it in the morning.

We don't actually make it to Matty's gaff as we bump into a lad I know from the homeless camps and go to a building that has been taken over as a squat. Prior to that I headed back to Strangeways! It is right across the road from Elysium and I had a tenner to get more spice that will sort me for the night as I already have a bit on me now.

The squat is an old bank and it has about forty of us in there, everyone is smoking spice and there are tents everywhere, apparently the building belongs to a footballer or someone like that. I am not arsed whose it is but I will crash here for now. I get talking to a sort of posh white lad with dreads about being in nick – "Yes mate, I was in Forrest Bank then they moved me to Strangeways cauz I was running the wing and had some trouble with some lads I knew from Liverpool," George lies to Andrew.

"Wow it must have been hard in there? I could not see myself losing my liberty, unless it was for something I believe in like the way homeless people are being abused by the Government right now!"

"It really sickens me, I mean my break down with my family has lead me to here, I could go back, but I feel I have some real work to do right now and make a difference."

I've heard this shit before and these lads come and go. At the minute he has an eighth of spice on him and we can chat all the shit in the world till it's gone.

I think I crash around four in the morning and I wake up around seven. I will go to the YPSF when it opens. I need to go to McDonald's first, I need the toilet... I think the spice is messing my stomach up.

6

Manchester

Mo

I get into Manchester at twelve o'clock, I snuck on to the train and spent most of the ride in the toilet, I don't care about the fine but I cannot be bothered with the hassle. I will not be reported missing from home until after eleven tonight so I don't really need to worry about being arrested by the feds. I get to the camps and speak to Ricky about what happened.

The camp is around two hundred metres from the town hall step. There are around thirteen tents all side by side and it is sheltered from the elements. It is approximately fifteen metres by fifteen metres and is officially a walk way in-between the big building that surrounds and shelters it. The camp shelter reminds Mo of the school he used to go to where the kids would store their bikes. Mo and his mate successfully stole numerous bikes from there; it was over a year until he was arrested and when he was convicted. It was taken into consideration that he was guilty of eight other bike thefts.

"Yes, Bro," says Ricky who is completely whacked on spice.

"Hiya Ricky, what's happening?" Mo says reservedly.

Ricky is known to be a bastard when he has no spice, which is rare to be honest but in the mornings everyone usually goes straight to Elysium as everything is gone from the night before so this could be a dangerous time to speak with Ricky, a 6ft tall, lean, young man. Mo is 5 ft 5 inches and has never been the best fighter but in a group he will lay into anyone no matter how tall. However the fact here remains, Ricky is the leader (he thinks he is anyway) although this is being tested by Vinnie more and more.

"Who's here?" asks Mo.

"Everyone; they're all crashed out though. Vinnie's at his dad's I think. I heard that George is out from a lad at Elysium."

Mo is pleased to hear this, George does not take the piss out of him for being young (fifteen) and he also does not wind him up for being stupid, in fact Mo thinks George is like himself. He was not good at school and is not the best reader or writer and was also in care. George says he does not need to read or write as he will make lots of money other ways so it will be sweet.

"Where is he? Do you know?" Mo eagerly asks Ricky.

"Not sure pal. He was with a lad and a girl who they didn't know. I am going to the YPSF and to life share to meet Kane; he might be there. Do you want to come?"

"Yeah," Mo instantly replies.

Ricky goes into his tent and mutters something to someone in there, he thinks it's a girl by the way he is speaking but does not ask him who it was. They set off to the YPSF going past the town hall. Ricky passes a joint to him. Mo thinks to himself the best thing about spice is that it can make time fly. – 5 hours can fly by like it was 30 minutes and the cold doesn't feel that bad. It is there, but it's not there, it's weird, but in a good way. I guess that's why it's legal.

7

YPSF

The Young People's Support Federation is on Oldham Street in the centre of Manchester. It offers support for young homeless people who are in crisis from the ages of 16-25. The building is over three floors and has approximately fifteen staff plus volunteers and several third year students who will do their placement there. The federation has been hit severely by the government cuts and they survive on 70% of the staff team they had previously. If it was not for the volunteers, students and support from other agencies who hire office space (space which was occupied by the redundant staff members!) they would not be able to offer service such as the breakfast drop in twice a week.

I have been sitting in here for half an hour and still not been sorted. The manager has been down to speak to me about intimidating the others and the way I speak to the staff.

"Hi Vinnie, look pal we are happy to support you but you will have to lower noise a bit and we cannot accept the language and tone of voice you are using to the staff and volunteers. People are here to support you but you're not making it easy for yourself and others," explains the YPSF manager, Steve Jones.

Vincent "Vinnie" Keane is a lean 5 ft. 10 inches, twenty year old young adult. His voice is deep and his manner is of manic-like behaviour. He has approximately twenty different scams & ideas in his head a second and they are forgotten and rethought continuously. His hair is usually shaven and jet black with a goatee beard and his eyes are dark brown. People sometimes question his ethnicity as mixed race, he is however white Irish born and raised in Cheetham Hill, Broughton which borders him as Mancunian and from Salford. Vinnie does like the idea as being seen as mixed race as it goes well for engaging with women for a reason he is not too sure of.

"All I am saying is I have been here ages and no one has come to see me. I will go outside and chill with them, but shout me when Sammy," – his YPSF housing case worker – "comes down." Vinnie does not wait for Steve's response; he goes out and expects to be called by the staff when they come down.

Vinnie goes outside and speaks with some of the YPSF service users who are outside and some older men who are accessing the Addiction Dependency Service which is an adult service directly across the road from YPSF. They are all smoking spice except Vinnie who rarely smokes spice. His drug of choice is cocaine but he only uses this when he is drinking alcohol. Vinnie has pride in his appearance and likes to think he looks the part at all times.

Whilst dominating the conversation of the young people outside the YPSF, Vinnie notices two lads approaching and immediately recognises Mo and Ricky. Oldham Street is deceivingly long and is sectioned off like the streets and avenues of New York leading up to Piccadilly Gardens. What looks like a two minute straight walk from top to bottom can actually take five minutes plus, you can see the gardens all the way down which tends to throw you off a little.

"YES, MO," shouts Vinnie from outside the YPSF. This can be heard by both Ricky and Mo and actually startles some of the hairdressers on their lunch break who are no doubt heading to Morrison's for the salad bar meal deal. Vinnie is loud; he knows this and displays it in any circle. His reaction to people who challenge or raise the fact is "I don't give a fuck" and he genuinely doesn't!

When Ricky and Mo eventually get to the YPSF, Vinnie and Ricky embrace each other with a 'man hug' then as in line of command he man hugs Mo.

"What the fuck happened to you. Mo?" asks Vinnie.

"The PCSO who always recognises me got me outside McDonald's in the square. These (YPSF) had reported me in the area when I saw that worker Joe on Sunday night. They sent me back to the care home in a van. Well, they actually drove me to Wigan first and then a police officer from Wigan drove me to the care home in a car."

"What you doing now, Vinnie?" Ricky asks.

"I am waiting on these to sort me out with some accommodation. I am sick of sofa surfing at me dad's and living in the tent. I have banged some clothes in their washing machine so I have got to get that sorted too. Where you off to?"

Ricky tells Vinnie he is to go and see Kane. Kane gets his benefits paid into Lifeshare's bank account. Lifeshare is a small charity set up for young homeless people and "rough sleepers". It allows you to have your benefits paid into their account if you are unable to have an account in yours. Kane did a cheque scam with the bank a few years ago and has been blacklisted from every high street bank in the country. He had seven grand put into his account; when the cheque cleared he received £2,000.00 and the lads took the remaining £5,000.00. He never saw the lads again after that; apparently they were doing the scam all over the country. It was a lad who he used to buy weed off who introduced him to the scammers.

8

Kaneyay

Kane is waiting at the door of Lifeshare. He like the others is completely high on spice. Kane is originally from South Manchester and has all the swagger of a black teenager of the 1990s when gangster rap was at its boom. Kane is white; he speaks with the dialect of "South Manchester" and really is lost to the reality of society. His step dad was sentenced to thirty years for the murder of a rival gangster when he was twelve. All that was left behind for his mum, himself and his two half-sisters was poverty, numerous house moves and the greatest vinyl collection of hip hop, Gangsta rap and Motown records you could ever wish for. The records are now pawned into a record shop near Affleck's Palace and the monies that have come from it are in Elysium!

"Safe yo! What you saying boys?" Kane greets the lads as a whole as they approach to meet him at Lifeshare. He raises his fist and touches each lad knuckle to knuckle on arrival.

"Safe, bro, what's been happening Kaneyay?" Vinnie calls Kane Kaneyay as in Kanye West as a piss take, however Kane actually thinks it is a compliment because of his ability to free style rap and cover tracks of Jay Z.

The weather is cold wet and grey, like any other day in Manchester. The lads want to go inside but there is spice to be smoked and this is paramount.

"I am just waiting for them to sort me money out, yo, then I am getting on it boys; blazing like a mo fo yo," says Kane.

With this, Colin comes down to the front door and asks Kane to come upstairs. This is good news for the lads as they know he will have money and will be stuck to him like the plague today.

Kane comes out with his money in hand; eyes still bloodshot red like everyone else in the group. When someone is stoned you can tell by their eyes and body movement. However, when someone is high on spice you can see the bright red blood vessels are almost pinkish in their eyes.

Spice was originally marketed as the cheap equivalent to cannabis – this is the biggest lie ever told! When on spice you look like a zombie from the film *I Am Legend*. When you actually smoke it the toxic levels in it shut you down like a lap top being updated and rebooted. The drug really is that strong. Its come down is nasty, the withdrawal is worse than heroin; in fact it is said to be harder to come off spice than heroin.

The boys head off back in the direction of YPSF and bump into George, this is turning out good. George is free, Kane has money, Mo is Mo, Ricky and Vinnie seem to be getting on… for now.

9

Mobile Phones

George

I am totally buzzing when I see my boys, none of 'em came to see me in jail like but obviously people are busy innit. My only visitors was Amy and Lee and that's shit, cannot talk to them about grafting; all they want to do is get me a job or on a traineeship or in supported accommodation. I don't want any of that. I got Lee off my case and told him I wanted to be a fitness instructor as I was doing bits in the nick, so he said he will research a course for me.

I asked him about a two bedroom flat as well, he turned to me straight away and said so you can grow cannabis in one room and sleep in the other. The fucker was right as well, apart from that I would sleep on the couch and grow in both rooms. Some lad there in the nick said he would set it all up for me and we can go 50/50 on the grow. I sometimes think Lee knows the score and is not just a straight head do-gooder.

Yes boys listen to this; I stayed at that bank squat last night and was talking to a hippie guy having a smoke like. When he fell asleep I went in his bag and took his passport and all his letters with his house address on it and his student passes. George is thinking about going to his home address and robbing it, however Vinnie has bigger plans.

"Let me see that ID."

George hands him the documents and Vinnie instantly texts his cousin to call him back. Within 5 minutes his cousin Sarah calls him back. Sarah works at the O2 store on Market Street; he fills her in on what he has got and the scam is on… Kane is not happy that he is not getting included in the cut and tells them he will meet them later he is going to Elysium. The boys are not bothered now as they feel they have a winning ticket and quickly get to Market Street. Vinnie opens two contracts in O2 with the latest iPhone, then he goes into the Vodafone store and gets two more contracts this time going for the new Samsung's and finally he goes into EE across the way and for two more phones … He wanted iPhones again as they sell quicker but there was a promotion for Samsung which gave the new tablet with every phone contract on a two year contract so he had to go with that. He felt it would be wrong not to. The whole scam took less than an hour and forty-five minutes as the shops are all together; from experience, Vinnie knows you have to do it in the day as after around six hours records come up on the screens and alarms bells start to ring.

Vinnie really enjoyed being Andrew Moir for the day and would like to shake the man by the hand if he ever meets him. Now it's off to Bury New Road to sell the gear. Good days don't come round like this often and with the January sales on Vinnie is thinking new trainers and trackies are getting bought whilst these muppets can smoke their share of the money.

"Fucking buzzing man we are getting dough out of this," says George, who is still intending to rob his house with Mo but that will be on the QT as Andrew gave his life story to him including his dad's long hours at the surgery, his mum in Marbella and sister at Edinburgh University. The kid's the best support worker he has ever had!

10

Spice of Life

Ricky

Vinnie does well with the phone scam and I have to give him credit for it, but trade is my speciality and I know exactly who to go to get rid of the goods straight away.

"Listen boys, we are not going to Elysium with the phones. Come with me to the end of Bury New Road, I have a contact who will sort the lot for us, but George and Mo will have to wait away from the shop as he is pretty paranoid. Vinnie is on the ball straight away and senses what I have lined up, a little cut for me and him and then split it four ways after."

"Why does Vinnie get to go with you?" asks George.

"Because I know the lad as well and I don't want him taking the piss or Ricky ripping us all off, you know I won't have that," says Vinnie.

This was good from Vinnie as he has thrown them off the scent straight away and obviously knows we have to have our separate cut from these two thick fuckers.

Me and Vinnie head off up the road leaving George and Mo outside Elysium chatting to some young girls we know that stay in a hostel called SAFE STAY in

Didsbury. We reckon that the gear is worth £3,200 brand new and want £1,500 at least.

We do the deal with Shazad from Umar Phones. He tries telling us the phones are not the new ones as the new ones come out next month and he will have trouble shifting them. He originally offered us £400 for the lot. Vinnie told him straight that he was going to have Preston burn the shop down for an eighth of spice and makes to leave out of the shop. Shazad laughs him off.

"Come on lads let's do a deal. Ricky you're a good lad and I will give £1,000 for the lot, take it or leave it. I have to get rid of these; it's not as easy as you think," explains Shazad.

I think he is full of shit as he is texting profusely whilst bartering with us. We walk out with £1,000 and we are not happy, but what the fuck can you do. We take £100 each then walk back to the boys.

"That Shazad is a dodgy guy Vinnie, he knows some serious people."

"I know but I also know how he got that shop and remember him from when he used to work at Sheepland Fashions at the back of the trading estate. I robbed the place years ago with my old mates and when the police arrived they found loads of heroin in there. The place was just a front for the trafficking business. He got away with the charges as he was just a young kid working there but the three owners got slammed. Apparently he had cashed in on the sheepskin coats when eBay was easy to trade on with no comebacks. He remembers me and I remember him. Fuck him."

When we get to Elysium the girls are sharing a joint with George and Mo. They are complaining that Jazz –

one of the owners – won't sell them Spice so George had to go in and buy it.

"What's the score?" says George.

"£800 for the lot," I lie.

Mo and George don't even question it; they are just buzzing to get £200.00 each.

We split the money, George and Mo get off, Vinnie says he is going into town then he will be in the Wetherspoons later and we agree to meet up there. I stay and speak with Jazz as I have an idea.

11

24 Hour Trading

Ricky

I ask Jazz why he will not sell to the girls. Jazz explains with that all the shit in the papers with Rotherham and Rochdale he thinks it's better to not have any of them near the shop.

"It looks like a high school playground around the shop most of the day," says Jazz. He has built a good business, so he does not really need that negativity that comes with it.

"Look, Jazz I have an idea. I have people coming to the camp all the time asking for spice in the night and early morning why don't we do a deal and I can sell to EVERYONE in town and you can still be making money when you are a sleep? You know I am not like these homeless fuckers. I am giving it up when it becomes illegal in a few months."

Jazz sees that I have a good idea and we do a deal, he tells me to box clever and not smoke into profits or into debt! It's not a warning, but it's the first time I have ever heard him speak to me straight, he is usually dead friendly with everyone.

Jazz is part owner of Elysium. He also sells legal highs on eBay and owns www.mcrlegalhighs.com www.legalhighsmanchester.com which ships legal highs internationally in twenty-four working hours. He also sells the "Annihilation 44" the UK's first home grown legal high which, if rumours are correct, is dried out Japanese knot weed with the legal high sprayed on it then the vape tobacco flavourings for taste and manufactured in the back of the shop by a chemist.

He has now just put his business firmly in the camps being sold 24/7. This may seem very *Breaking Bad* but the demand is there and he has been hoping for a mug like Ricky to start to work for him 24/7 on a good month he can go through a 10 kilo box of spice imported from Eastern Europe.

Jazz was looking to identify someone who has a bit of bullying power about them in the camps and at the same time been completely hooked to spice. Ricky is the perfect candidate. Now he just needs another two more and he reckons he will profit £2,000 a week from it. Jazz is also aware of the likelihood spice will be made illegal. Going off the news reports, he gives it another year max so he also thinks it's better to start early in shifting the kids away from the shop. Very soon they will not bother coming and he will only have a handful of customers from the camps, as he will not serve them and that will direct them straight to Ricky. He weighs up the hazards too. Ricky going to jail for a crime or losing his mental health, which will happen to him as it HAS done to everyone else. He just hopes he does not lose it completely as it could cost Jazz money. He really wants

the new Mercedes, he has set his mind to it now and he
WILL get it.

12

The Morning After

It's freezing outside. George's feet are like ice, tracing about the city in the cold and wet makes his feet permanently wet and the cold is bitter He slept in the tent with Mo and cannot really remember last night as they were in a mess. He checks his pockets and feels he still has some money and is relieved to feel a bag of spice too.

George does not own a mobile phone or a watch; he does not know what time it is but he can hear the city is awake, the cars, the people walking past the tents. He can hear stilettos clicking on the street and men talking about the game last night. He thinks this must mean it is morning or lunch time. Usually he could tell by the temperature or by the daylight. In spring and summer it is light outside and the temperature goes up in the afternoon but in the dead of winter it is still dark at eight a.m. but light for eight thirty but the temperature never changes.

"You awake, Mo?" George says quietly.

Mo sits up without saying anything. He goes out of the tent to get a drink. In the city, people always leave their drink or half of their sandwich at the tents; it's become a norm or a trend among the city workers. Prior to the up rise of the homeless people in Manchester you would probably see the odd quid given into a begging cup on Friday afternoon or people righteously buying the *Big Issue*. Nowadays, to be homeless and hungry is rare. There is always food available. Some of the trendy eateries in the Northern Quarter have a soup kitchen that prides its self on the 'Posh Nosh' it serves up.

Mo finds a half bottle of Sprite. It's freezing cold but he does not care, he guzzles it down and saves some for George. Vinnie can be heard on his phone in the next tent, the Polish people are talking to each other from inside their tents, cans of beer can be heard being pierced open. Mo cannot fathom how the Polish group can drink all day every day and never seem drunk? Ricky appears out of the tent his black hooded top is over his face and his scarf is pulled down as he has a joint that is ready to be lit.

"Alright Mo," says Ricky. His voice is hoarse and he can hear the girl from the other day asking him to pass the joint to her first.

Who is this girl? Mo wonders.

Safe, bro, top day yesterday, where did youse get to?" asks Mo.

"We were in Wetherspoons with Kane."

"Why was Vinnie screaming at everyone? I could hear him but I was wrecked and could not make sense?" Vinnie quickly interrupts Mo.

"I WENT FOR A PISS LAST NIGHT AND ONE OF YOU DIRTY BASTARDS HAVE SHIT THERE."

At the side of the camp is a small ally and everyone in the camp uses it to pee, even the girls on camp. It is kind of agreed that if you need to go to the toilet for a number 2 you go to the McDonalds around the corner.

"I WAS FUCKED OUT OF MY FACE AND COULD NOT SEE A THING IN THE ALLY AND DID NOT KNOW I STOOD IN IT UNTIL I GOT IN THE TENT WHEN I COULD SMELL THE SHIT ON MY TRAINERS I EVEN HAVE IT IN HERE IT FUCKING STINKS ITS NOT EVEN FUCKING DOG SHIT!!!!!"

Vinnie is really annoyed. I can see his new Nike Huaraches at the side of the tent with human shit up the side of them.

"IF I FIND OUT WHO HAS DONE THIS YOU ARE FUCKING DEAD."

With that, Vinnie puts his new shit-ridden trainers on, throws his JD sports bag over his shoulder and leaves the camp. I note that I do want the new grey tracksuit he has bought, it's smart.

The "girl" finally puts her head out of the tent. I know her; well I know who she is, it's Janey. Janey used to live at Safe Stay when George was there.

"Hiya Mo, are you ok?"

"Hiya Janey when did you come here?"

Janey is a big spice user and loves spice! About eight months ago she started selling it to the people who lived in Safe Stay youth hostel with her ex-boyfriend Nate. Within five weeks EVERYONE was on it. The staff could even identify the smell it was that bad in there. This is what George has told me anyway. The thing is with Janey we both have a secret, well sort of, I know what she does and she knows what I have done we would not talk about it, but I think she knows or thinks what I think.

13

Janey

Janey is known as "damaged goods" in several areas of the city. Her plight to the tents (this is her second stint) started in a good family home. Janey has one sister and two brothers; she is the second born in her family. She has a younger brother and sister. During Euro 96 in Manchester, Janey's Dad, Mike Hudson a hardworking man, joiner by trade but could put his hand to anything died by choking on his own vomit in his sleep the same night England beat Scotland and the IRA bomb hit the city. Mike was twenty-nine years old. Janey was just two years old. Mike left behind his devoted wife Claire (a part-time dinner lady and cleaner at the school). His son Mikey Junior was eleven years old and the twins were one year old.

The pathway plan was to buy a house and Mike had dreams of his own van and his own company. From the tragedy that hit the house lead to a severe breakdown for mum, which stopped her from ever working again and she took to drinking and Prozac (a new drug on the NHS in England and Scotland). The children rarely attended school apart from Mikey Junior for whom, on reflection, his father's death was a pivotal point and he went on to live a successful life in London moving on to Cornwall where he currently is now.

Eight years after her father's death, Claire Hudson was "seeing" a local bloke from the area Steve Gallagher. They had been a couple for around eighteen months and they shared a turbulent relationship; both had a passion for drink, and had mental health issues. One night during another late house party Janey came downstairs after hearing Steve and his drinking partner Terry Bolton arguing. As she got to the bottom of the stairs she heard a scuffle, a thud and then an eerie silence! When Janey opened the door Steve had a blade in his chest. He died at the scene. Janey had the traumatic experience of not only witnessing this but also having to testify in court. This was the beginning of a downward spiral for Janey. Within six months after the trial she was on a care order of the council to reside in a private children's care home in Openshaw. In the beginning she hated being away from her mum (although she could stay at home at weekends) but she did enjoy the fact she was bought nice clothes, given spends and had nice cooked food, this was only a vague memory of her former upper working class family home.

Janey was also introduced to smoking bud (cannabis); she smoked cigarettes but not cannabis, especially this type. She has seen her mam with a chocolate type lump that she burned into her roll up, but this stuff was different and had a super strong smell.

In her first six month in care she had lived in two different care homes, started to smoke cannabis daily and had lost her virginity and became sexually active. At fourteen, her link worker wanted her to go on the contraceptive pill and had genuine concerns regarding her not practicing safe sex. Janey refused to allow her link worker to discuss this with her mum as Janey was not on a full care order the staff could not make the decision and had to get mum's permission. The facts are Janey has her right to stop them from discussing with mum as she did not want to disclose she was having sex. Janey was pregnant at fourteen, she also contracted genital herpes during her pregnancy and had the baby taken from her right after birth. The father of the child was never disclosed but staff thought it was one of the other boys who live in the four bedroomed home with her. At sixteen, Janey had been in three different schools she had been appointed a drug and alcohol support worker, she had lived in nine different care homes and was diagnosed as suffering with long term depression. Without going into too much detail of the four years in care homes she had been through some real tough times and left her childhood by the time she was fourteen.

Janey left her supported / independent living home at seventeen years and three hundred and fifty five days. She moved into an all-girls youth hostel. Three months after she was evicted from the all-girls supported accommodation for numerous fights, breaking all house rules and complete disregard for anyone who was in her world; to put it bluntly, she did not care for anyone, including herself. From here she moved into "safe stay" in the Didsbury area of Manchester, then her after care worker who she met once a week and gave her support for the next three years. Janey really hit a low in Safe Stay, she did not pay her rent, and here she was introduced to SPICE from Nate, the love of her life!

14

Court

George

It was around four a.m. when the Feds lifted me. I was arrested for an attempted house burglary in west Didsbury. I was allegedly meant to have tried entry via the back door. They have taken my trainers as evidence.

Detective Inspector Dave Braithwaite is doing the interview. I know him from another thing a year or so back where I got off with it.

"Can you tell us where you was on the afternoon of Friday 6th Feb at 16:45?"

"No comment."

"Is this you on CCTV at fifteen forty-five walking down Orchard Street West?"

"No comment."

This goes on for about ten minutes and obviously I know they have got me but I am not letting on, I think they have lifted Mo as well, but they are saying nothing. My solicitor arrives and speaks with the police. The police disclose that I have left my blood on the glass panel I broke. I'M FUCKED!! I am also to be remanded in custody to appear in court in the morning regarding the original suspended sentence for affray, breach of probation and not meeting Lee.

They give me a brew at eight a.m. and tell me I am first up at ten a.m. Obviously I am not arsed now, I am getting slammed for breaching my probation and conditions of the court plus the attempted burglary, and this will be referred to the Crown. My solicitor arrives just after nine a.m. and explains that I will be remanded as it is the same judge – Judge Brown – who gave me the suspended sentence!

"FUCK… What will happen about the new charge?"

"They have your DNA and you are allegedly shown on CCTV. My view is that the CCTV is insubstantial, but how do we explain your DNA on the glass panel door?"

"I'm not arsed. I will just go guilty and explain I was just knocking at my mates…"

George goes silent as he realises this could then link them to the phone scam. Either way he knows it is going to be a custodial.

"I will go guilty and they can sentence me whenever. I am not arsed."

When I get up to the dock I see Lee is in there, how the fuck does he know I am here already? The judge is in no mood. He accepts my guilty plea and sends me back down to complete my suspended sentence and I will be sentenced for the attempted burglary at a later date when the Pre-Sentence Report is done. Back to Forrest Bank it is for me.

15

Ricky

Ricky always has been one who falls in love easy. He has a very jealous streak which has ended all his relationships, especially the one with her. Leah the beautiful model from a good home, nice family all the things you could ask for in a girl. Ricky is thinking about how he is here and when he was there: happy, no problems, the sun on his face, the girl he loved, the job, the car, the weed. Everything was good. EVERYTHING

I'm stalking her profile on Instagram again; she is home now, back from the job on the ships as a dancer. It looks like she has a fucking boyfriend on her photos. I am blocked on Facebook but she does not know about my fake Insta profile. This lets me see her. It's been over two years now, well, we split two and half years ago, but we was still "seeing" each other for a bit afterwards. I just smoked weed then and played on the PlayStation in my room and then used to go to hers after I had seen my boys. We used to argue a lot about lads I think she was seeing or fancied. In the beginning it was brilliant, I could not believe a girl like her would like someone like me, off a council estate, a weed head. It was amazing; I would do anything for her. I just could not believe it. We were always together but then she started to want to go out with her mates more and she said I was too protective and she felt like I was too much! I was too much? She was the one who came to my house every day even bought me a phone so we could be in touch all the time! She asked for a break and I agreed to chill it as I was busy with my boys and knew I could see her for sex and I also had a couple of birds off the estate I was seeing too. We ended up having big kick off because she friended a guy I hate on Facebook. It was the final straw I went round and had a massive row. I hit her then her dad started, I hit him a few times and then I lost it. I put the house windows through, smashed her car up and was arrested. I was sent to Forrest Bank then Barnard Castle. This was the first time I had SPICE. It was brilliant. A day flew by on spice, serious it could be like one o'clock and you look at the telly in your pad and Coronation Street is on. Spice made time fly and I loved the high it gives me and still do!

When I got out of the nick I was not ready for what happened; trying to get off spice was the worst pain withdrawal I have ever known. I lasted five days and I swear they were the worst five days of my life. My pad mate warned me he said that he was on heroin for five years and in and out of nick for all five of them years. He got off heroin as his spice addiction was stronger... SPICE it calls you from your deepest depths and if you ignore it then it sends out your worst demons and makes them feel like yesterday. Nightmares you have had as a child, acts of violence you have seen that sickened you, memories of family funerals! You name it, the devil known as spice regurgitates it and amplifies your pain, hurt and fears – they all come back to life in 3D.

I heard that it takes four weeks to come off the withdrawal and you sweat constantly, shiver, shake and shit. Lee has told me there is one place that has a detox programme for it in Prestwich but the waiting time for it is months and the funding will be spent soon, they just cannot keep up with the volume of referrals. I am not ready yet, that's why I cannot see my mam or any of my mates, not like this NO WAY! I don't want them to think I am like these fuckers I AM NOT!

So I am here in this tent with Janey. She sleeps a lot of the day; in fact Janey sleeps more hours than anyone I have ever known that is homeless. I sleep around five hours a day in broken spells, probably less now since I have started to sell spice. The selling has gone really well, me and her don't have to pay for any spice any more as the lads off this camp alone bring in plenty, plus Preston and his pal Joel are here every day morning and night, they might as well stay here than on the third floor of the Arndale car park. It is a good spot though I will give 'em that.

16

The Drop In

Vinnie wakes up from his dad's couch. He can feel the heat on his face and he is sweating in the two pairs of tracksuit bottoms he is wearing. The gas fire has been left on all night, the fire was fitted by the council years ago and should have been changed, but to be fair it gives off more heat than the sun and you can rest your brew on it, not like the new ones they put in nowadays all slender and "compact fitted" like a TV on the wall. Vinnie's dad still has a big metal fire guard around the fire, this is not to protect the kids: the guard is perfect for hanging your clothes on to dry, especially jeans. The guard has actually come in to use for its actual design many times over the years when Vinnie Senior has fallen onto it or passed out into a drunken coma.

It's seven a.m. on his phone. Vinnie never sleeps so late he thinks he fell asleep watching *Match of the Day 2* on BBC 2 this means he must have had close to eight hours sleep, a record for him. He does seem to sleep well on that couch lately, longer than in the bed to be honest and especially down at the camps; it's freezing at the minute and it's looking like winter will never leave and he can only manage three or four nights a week down there. His dad's house makes him nauseous, but he seems to settle a lot easier in the flat. It is madness with them all being off their head all day and night. That fucking Ricky thinks he's Juan Pablo Escobar at the minute because the guy from Elysium has got him cuffed selling spice 24/7 to every user in Manchester, but I will play the game with that cunt, he has a few quid at the minute and will always get the beer in.

I decide to get up have a wash and brush my teeth. There is no food in the flat or any milk for a brew, so I head into town to the camps, catch up with the lads and we can all go to the drop in at YPSF for breakfast and a cuppa.

When I get there I notice that the camp area is a fucking tip, well it's always a tip, but something has gone on?

"YES BOYS WHAT A GWON," I shout to let them know I am here.

There is silence at first then Kane puts his head out of the tent, which no longer has no door on it.

"Yes pal," says Kane.

"–You missed last night pal, Janey and Ricky kicked off like fuck Janey smashed all the tents in and Ricky was punching the walls with his bare hands, I think he has broke both hands and his wrist."

"Where is he?" enquires Vinnie.

"Fuck knows. He went to the hospital with Preston and has not been back."

"And where's SHE?" Vinnie asks.

Kane looks towards the facing tent and nods his head at the tent distastefully. Vinnie pauses and thinks about Janey… She is not liked at all by the group and since she has been on the camp there have been fights, arguments and a general loss of harmony since her arrival. There is a business couple who drop off £50 or so nearly every week. This gets split to the camp. Recently, the couple have not been coming and suspicions are that Janey has manipulated them both to meet her separately and claim the money. No one can manipulate people with a conscience who want to do a good deed better than kids who have been in care and Janey is the crème de la crème of this kind!

Vinnie, Mo and Kane head off for breakfast at the YPSF. There is a lad called Joel who is also at the camp who Vinnie does not like. He sees himself as a local celebrity because he was on Granada News a few months ago. He went to the court to protest about the camp evictions in the city and had a very good solicitor from the charity Shelter behind him. The thing is, he won a right to remain for around four months and the media was all over this and Joel got recognised by everyone and made considerable financial gains from it via Joe Public, which he shared with no one, except Jazz from Elysium of course.

The breakfast club starts at ten and finishes at twelve. It was originally used as a way to engage the young people who are rough sleepers and enables the staff to monitor the mental and physical wellbeing. It is now a place for all the rough sleepers 16-25 years old in the city to have a good spice session together outside the front door then back in to get warm and eat free food and drink nice brews. The staff team who deliver the drop in are volunteers and students; it used to be the proper staff team but since the cuts they cannot cover it, so the young people just rule the roost!

When I walk in to the reception the usual suspects are here... a well presented lad and a girl. I don't think they are together, but they both have that same traumatised look that says "my mam and dad have kicked me out and I am shitting myself I have nowhere to go". If they only know the truth that lies ahead of them, I want to say to them both 'GO HOME BACK TO YOUR MIDDLE CLASS SEMI AND GET OVER WHATEVER BULLSHIT YOU AND YOUR FOLKS OR SIBLINGS HAVE AND GET ON WITH THE HAPPY LIFE AND FORTUNE YOU HAVE BEEN BORN INTO!' They would not listen to me even if I said it and I cannot blame them, to be honest who am I, Jeremy Kyle? Then there is the young pregnant girl... this one is in for a big shock, it will be around two years before she sees her own flat. Baby or not you're just not priority any more, girl. Finally, there are a couple of what I am guessing to be Somali's, there is no shock or trauma in their eyes, nothing this city can throw at them can go above the shit they probably have had to endure. They both just sit there in amazement at the herd of psychotic / manic young lads with zombie eyes that have walked through the door.

I say hello to Dave on reception and sign me, Mo and Kane in. I look on the sign in sheet. Ricky Jenkins, Preston Jones, Louis Hardy and Joe McCabe. Let the party begin!

17
Urban Village

Vinnie

When we walk through to the YPSF kitchen I can see the lads are completely off their face; Ricky is sweating like I have never seen before and both his hands are wrapped up in bandages, he looks like a boxer.

"What's happened to you?" I ask. Ricky looks bad!

"I was arguing with that bitch it was hit her or hit the walls, so I hit the walls and I think the CID might be looking for me because I smashed some bloke in the face and tried to bite his nose off, I lost it mate," Ricky says.

I can see the fear and paranoia building up in him the come down from this will be bad, however something tells me he will not come down for a week as he will be high as a kite for a while rather than face the pain of his hands and the reality of what his life has become, I find it hard to keep the smile off my face. One of the student girls comes over with the novice concerned look on her face and ask Ricky what is wrong.

"Are you okay? What happened?"

I quickly jump in – "He's the national under 23 British boxing champion love, just a sparring thing he will be fine in a couple of days."

She looks unconvinced, but the cold silence from us leads her to walk away mumbling something like I am here if you need me.

Lee walks in to the drop in and comes over to us, this fucker is too experienced to jump all over the Ricky thing, in fact he ignores it and starts speaking with Kane who can barely put food in his mouth off his fork he is that wasted. This spice is so fucking strong and the lads are all saying that they have changed the spice with something as it tastes different. I wouldn't know as I have only been smoking a couple of months but I have been feeling dizzy and nauseous recently when smoking it at my dad's house.

"Have you all got your benefits sorted out lads?" says Lee.

"Are your sick notes all in date?" Lee pretty much knows when our sick notes run out and is advising us all to go and get another month's note.

The government just stops all your benefits the minute you don't sign on, your sick note runs out or you cannot show any evidence you have been looking for a job. Our only fight back is to stay on the sick and go to the urban village doctors that do a walk in for the homeless in Ancoats. Ricky is guaranteed a sick note today for sure and some good pain killers too, but that's not what we need now. We all take a couple of Kane's tablets, I forget the name but they are like Temazepam. They make you drowsy as fuck at first but mixed with the spice leave you fucked up in a horrendous way. The quack has signed the sick note before your arse hits the chair; he wants us out of there ASAP.

18

Preston

Preston has, for lack of a better phrase, "gone to the game". Today he is happy as a pig in shit as he will be rolling all Ricky's joints as he cannot move his hands. No one is more of a slave in this world to legal highs than him. He has been kicked out of his mum's house by her bastard of a boyfriend. Preston's mum is also addicted to spice too. This makes for a volatile relationship for them both. His mum never really wanted him and has never really shown him love; he was officially in care as kid but always went back to his mum's and he brought cannabis with him, which was both his mum's and Preston's choice of drugs prior to the introduction of spice. Now like a genetic makeup both mum and son are attached to the drug like a fly stuck on one of the yellow sticky tapes you see in a kitchen, there is no way they are getting off it.

I walk in to the doctor's room and stare at him in the eye, but he looks at the computer like I am scaring him, I don't know why. He asks me how I am and I tell him about how spice has had the recipe changed.

"I smoke the Annihilation 44, doctor. It's better than the other spice, but it's different, not like mamba and chronic, like different to me and I need more of it than I do on the other stuff, you need to smoke some to understand?"

The doctor seems to shiver when I say this.

"How would you describe your mental health at the minute, do you feel the same as you felt last month or is there any improvement?"

People keep backing off when I am talking to them and Sammy has got Steve from the YPSF to come down to talk to me about people's personal space, but I know I am not right. It's the spice, everything's different now it's easier to be homeless and addicted to it than it would be living in a house it's too much to handle with the drug need I have got. The doctor gives me a month's sick note and I walk outside. We always wait outside as you cannot smoke inside, they threatened to ban me from the doctors for smoking in the door way.

Ricky has been given some really strong pain killers and we are all given a prescription for our "depression". Some of us have different stuff but this time I am given something different, he also asked if I have a support worker, I don't have one like the rest of them as I was not about when their programme started, I was about but just using the YPSF. It's gutting really because they get a bus pass and a mobile phone bought and if they meet up they get to go to Maccy Ds I see them sometimes going in the new one in Piccadilly. The guy Lee gets me a drink and sandwich when he sees me begging outside near the cash machine. The doctor wants me to have an assessment and said he wants to refer me or something, he has given me a card to go to a place but I won't go.

We head off to the job centre and I am happy making Ricky's joints and we get some beer to walk up with; none of us really drink, it is just Vinnie he likes a drink and told me I would be sorted for spice if I nick a crate out of the Tesco, so I did, but I am not happy about having to carry it.

19

The Visit

George

I am in my pad and told I have a visit, it's a professional visit so it can only be my solicitor, Amy, Lee or the CID. I get in the room and I can see Lee with the life-is-good smile across his boat race, but he drops this as soon as he can see I am wrecked and goes into his "I'm concerned" look that I have seen a thousand times before by a hundred or more workers just like him. Professional visits are shit, not just for the bullshit conversations, but you cannot have a brew or a biscuit in this nick, in Doncaster you could.

"How are you matey?" says Lee.

"I'm alright me, but obviously it's shit in here, can you send me a postal order?"

"I have sent it today and my line manager says I can send £10 a month is that ok? If Amy can send you one as well and you get a job in here you should be okay for your toiletries, tobacco and sweets."

"I owe money for burn and I am in a bit of shit."

"What have you done, mate?" His tone changes to one that was prepared for something.

"I got caught with a parcel the other day in the laundry. It had four phones, 1oz of burn and 2oz of spice!" George informs him and goes on to add the bigger problem.

"I also have been found with a bladed article in my cell."

"A knife? When was this? You have only been in here ten days."

"The gear was not mine and the knife was a toothbrush with a razor blade melted on it; it was to open the parcel not to stab anyone. I am in a segregation unit now. They are going to charge me with me with smuggling the gear into the nick and possession of a bladed article. I'm fucked but I'm not arsed. Apparently I may never be able to have a pad mate because of the blade; I am considered a danger to other inmates. Some of the lads are saying I can get two years if the nick takes me to court or the governor can charge me from in here with it, it depends on my outcome of my burglary sentence? My solicitor came in and said that obviously it was not mine as I was only in here forty-eight hours before getting caught with it and the only person I have contacted on the outside is him with when I rang him."

Lee is almost speechless but does agree with my solicitor.

"George, why are you taking the shit for others in here pal? You know you will be the one who ends up with the wrap."

"Are you on Spice now?"

I nod.

"How have you got it?"

I don't answer but he knows I am plugging the spice and phones again for a lad in here.

"Lee. You don't know how much money can be made in here on spice, it's a fucking fortune mate and I get sorted for minding it. You can compress an ounce of spice to the size of the orange tip on a cig and the phones are really small, have you not seen them for sale on Bury New Road – they are tiny and I know what I am doing as well."

Lee's eye squint like he is reading the Newspaper, he changes the subject.

"What did the solicitor say about your sentencing?"

"He reckons in all I will do five months if the Pre-Sentence Report goes well for me we are waiting on that and then a date so if all is well I can be out in August."

"Then what?" Lee firmly says.

"You have been in prison to the street and back three times now and have refused to take any support from me if we are honest. What do you want George, do you not want a home, a job a life?"

I just shrug at him and look at the floor.

"Do you think you could do twenty years in prison like the lifers?" Lee asks with intrigue.

"What happens happens, obviously I don't want to but if it does it does," replies George.

Lee stares off over George's head for a second and thinks he is the most institutionalised young person he has ever met in fifteen years of youth support work. He genuinely does not care if he spends his life in prison; the real sad truth is he probably will not live to see thirty years of age and his funeral will have no family there and possibly no friends to attend either.

Lee changes the subject and goes on about Manchester City playing someone in Champions League. I don't like football, I have told him this; I like rugby as I used to play a bit. I also like playing table tennis, it really gives me a relaxing feeling after playing, I tell him this and he starts going on about some report that it is good for post-traumatic stress disorder. He always tries to revert to this with me and wants me to have some counselling. The screw knocks on the window and says it is time to go.

"That went quick?"

"I know pal. I was waiting for you for nearly half an hour in this room, what happened?"

"Fuck all, I was in my pad and they come and took me straight to you?"

Lee tells me to be careful and he will be back in two weeks and will ask Amy to come and see me then gets off.

20
Supported Accommodation

Vinnie

I have been hitting the beer and the spice the last week. Staying in these tents you cannot get away from it. The English lads surround me with Spice and the Polish lads surround me with strong lager. Not that I am complaining, but a week in the tents you need to detox; it's hard work, I mean if it was easy everyone would do it, wouldn't they?

I have to go and see Sammy at the YPSF. Sammy is my worker, but Steve sits in now. I think I intimidate her a bit, but these students need to toughen up or ship out. Sometimes it's like I'm their social worker when I explain it to them that they are in a crisis zone, there will be conflict, especially when I need a place to stay and I am "manic".

I gets to the door and the new reception guy lets me in and gets on the phone as I go through the door. He has a look in his face like he is reporting DEFCON 5 to the Pentagon! I must have caused a bit of shit the other day, it's all a bit vague as I have been a bit blitzed!

Steve comes down.

"Alright Steve, where's Sammy?"

"Hello Vinnie. She's not here today, mate, can I have a word I have some news for you."

We go into the meeting room, which is the size of the toilet in my mate's 1940s council house. 3 foot wide by 6 foot long, you know the ones where you would lose your knee caps off the door if someone barges in and you're having a dump. Anyway, Steve tells me I have an interview today at Elizabeth house in Clayton and I have to be there for eleven a.m. He gives me the money for the bus fare and off I go. I know Elizabeth House; I've been here a few times with the boys. It's supported accommodation and the ages range from 17-45 and the people in there are usually crack heads or complete piss heads. Both have no way of return and are destined to see out their life there or get kicked out for non-payment of the rent or "service charge" as they call it.

My pal who lived here last time I was here had to leave as he got a job and could not afford the fucking rent. You see, the rent is £249 a week in supported accommodation, plus the service charge which ranges from £12 to £17 a week so if you are on benefits, the social will pay the £249 and you pay the £17 quid, but if you're on Employment Support Allowance like me or worse, Job Seekers Allowance it is around a third of your money. No one pays it you just keep in debt until it goes to something like £400 and then they kick you out. They say you're out after 3 weeks but you never are. I don't know a single person who has lived in supported accommodation or is living in supported accommodation that is not in rent arrears. I hear Janey managed to get her rent arrears service charge up to £1980 quid in Safe

Stay and that is because the housing benefits team suspended her for not going to her JSA appointment because she was too fucked to get out of bed and get a sick note from the doctors. So she was down £249 for each of the two week, add this to her six months of not paying her service charge of £17 a week. It's a vicious game this benefits thing nowadays.

Anyway, as I say my mate Terry, he got a job labouring, cards in, so his housing benefit stopped straight away. He came out with £285.00, they wanted £261.00 rent a week leaving him with £24 to live on and he had bus fares to pay out of that. He fucked it off, got back on the beer and was evicted three weeks later in rent arrears and is now unable to bid on a council flat as he is in arrears and has not made a payment plan! Fucking blacklisted for going to work, what has the world come to. Thinking about all this has got me FUMING I have to have a cig and calm down before I go in. Some rat of a human asks me for a cig, tries and tries to sell me crack on her way out of the building. I tell her to fuck off very loud which makes the staff all look out of the window. Boy I am FUMING. *Calm down VIN, calm down* I say to myself.

I have the interview with the woman; she's in her early 50s although it could be early 30s with the job she is in. I don't know how they fucking do it day after day. Anyway, it goes well and as all my benefits are in place and Steve has emailed them putting me as priority I am offered a place to stay. I cannot fucking believe it, this does not happen. You usually go on the waiting list for about a two months or longer then you miss your appointment when they call you as you are homeless and mobile numbers are changed weekly when you are homeless for numerous reasons. Anyway, fuck it I have a gaff and I am going to my dad's to get my shit.

When I gets to my dad's house he is not answering I bang on the door.

"DAD IT'S VINNIE!"

I know he is in as the telly is on I can hear it.

"DAD, OPEN THE FUCKING DOOR!"

Something in my stomach tells me something is wrong. I climb over the metal railings and get into the back area of the flat and climb up the veranda of the ground floor and grip onto a six inch piece of pipe hanging off the bottom of our veranda on the first floor. The pipe is for draining the water that builds up from the rain, I then lift onto the top of the concrete wall and pull myself up. I can see through the window that the fire is on and he is on the couch, my senses say he is not sleeping.

The door is not locked, it rarely is I walk in and call him softly, probably the first time I have ever spoke to him in this tone, as I walk past the back of the couch I can see his face, closed eyes and he is pale. What the fuck! My dad is DEAD. I nudge him with my hand; he is not moving. I can see he is gone. It must take about five minutes before I move I open the door and knock on to Enid's door facing my dad's.

"Enid, can you call an ambulance please for my dad."

Enid does not get chance to open her mouth, Strangely I am not shouting or feeling my usual rage, I am calm sort of tranquil I cannot explain it.

"What's happened Vincent, is he okay?"

71

"No, Enid. He's gone," I say. With that the tears begin to roll.

21

Contraception

Janey

The winter is going and coming back and going, it's not been a bad one there was a few cold nights but this year was not too bad, just a long one. Today is my birthday: March 23rd. I am 21 years old.

"Ricky, are you awake?" Janey calls out to Ricky. He has been sleeping heavier since he has been on the new medication. She has been serving the camp's spice through the night for the last couple of weeks.

"What, yeah what time is it?"

"I don't know, the phones are dead."

Ricky gets up and immediately puts his hand out towards Janey, who passes him the joint filled with the toxin they love known as SPICE.

"I have to go and see my mum today, will you come with me?"

"No, I am staying here and I have got to go and see Jazz, what's left from last night did anyone come?"

"Preston came with Joe. Joel was here with Naomi."

"Who's Naomi?" asks Ricky.

"You don't know her, she's been staying at the bank place, but everyone's getting kicked out of it and they was supposed to be getting put in a flat or hostel but it's all been a load of lies. Apparently the council was lying and Lakeside Housing Trust said all along they could not put them all in their flats and hostels. They are in the tent across. I am going to McDonalds to charge the phone do you want anything?"

"No, I'm okay." Ricky flicks the joint and throws some waste outside the camp. *It's getting really bad round here for mess* he thinks to himself, *the dirty bastards.*

Janey puts her trainers on and sprays some of the deodorant on her clothes and goes out of the tent. She calls to Naomi and another girl named Jody who has moved on to the camp with her fella. Jody is actually still in care like Mo, but her fella, Mark has been evicted from Safe Stay for non-payment of rent and a few warnings so she is here with him now.

The girls walk to McDonalds on St. Anne's Square Janey gets three coffees and tell the girls she is going out tonight as it is her birthday.

"Are you on the pill, Janey?" asks Naomi.

"No, are you?"

"No," she says.

"My periods are all messed up sometimes I skip sometimes I get them twice, I am messed up at the minute," explains Janey.

All three girls look at each other and it transpires that they have the same issues. Naomi explains about what a couple of girls were talking about at the squat.

"None of us are on anything and we all have smoked spice for over a year. My periods are messed up like yours and weirdly like the girls at the bank squat."

"What are you saying?" asks Janey.

"Do you think the spice is stopping us getting pregnant, like the pill? Do you think it's weird that NO ONE we know is having a baby?"

Janey thinks about this for a second and has a flash back from a conversation she had with the nurse at the clinic. The nurse explained to her that there may be a link but the staff team was concerned that it may make them infertile and even after giving up spice they may not be able to have children.

Currently there is no research to support this as there is no funding. The data collected from the users is they are not getting pregnant, although they are sexually active. The first theory is that the women users are not getting pregnant because of their diet and it cannot be conclusive that it is the toxins making them unable to reproduce. Another question currently being asked is: is it the women who are having fertility issues or is it the men? Does spice make both men and women infertile, reduce fertility or have no effect? Due to several services being hit by government cuts no one can explain or give accurate answers other than the users.

"I want more kids, I know this. They took my baby off me when she was born I will never forgive them for that that fucking slag of a social worker and the care home staff they never even give me a chance, my little girl would be nearly seven now." Janey's eyes water as she says this but no tears fall, she has shed more tears in the last five years than any time in her life and when she

75

thinks back, she shed a lot of tears through childhood too!

"My mum looks after my son, but she will not let me even see him. I went to jail after he was born and she got custody of him. All they will offer me is one hour every month at a shitty family centre!" Naomi explains her child dilemma. "I know he is safe with her but she is so evil to me, she's the reason I am here living like this."

"I don't have children; I don't think I will ever want them especially when I am like this and I am only 16!" Jody speaks with confidence about her thoughts on being a mother and her honesty to herself shows some ambition that she will get back on track one day.

"Last Sunday was fucking horrible, I mean mother's day is horrible for everyone who is homeless but for us mothers it hurts more," Janey moans.

"I did not even lift my head from the tent. I was wasted all day and just could not face it. Ricky knew what was up with me and was nice for a bit to be fair."

Janey gets up and orders a breakfast whilst she waits for the phones to charge. Naomi and Jody go outside to smoke the joint that they put out on entering McDonalds. The girls have no money for food, they are not hungry and the thought of food in the morning makes them both nauseous.

22

A New Home

Mo

I got lifted at the YPSF and taken to a new care home in Wythenshawe. This is good for me as I don't have to keep getting taken back to Wigan. This home is bigger and has six kids in here and an extra care worker on shift. I am gonna stay a couple of days to see what it is like then I am off back to the boys. I am introduced to the care home manager. Sue is a big white woman who smells nice and dresses smart.

"Hi Mohammed, it says on your file you like to be called Mo, can I call you Mo?"

"Yeah," I say in a low mumble I keep my eyes fixed to the floor as I cannot be bothered with the routine introduction to the home as I have been here before.

"Do you want to come out with me today to the Trafford Centre to get you some new clothes and trainers and we can also get you some toiletries and have something to eat while we are out?"

I lift my head up. I want some new trainers bad, my feet are always soaked and I have big holes in these. I also want that tracky Vinnie has as well.

"Yeah I'm not bothered."

I want them clothes but I am not letting them know this; I am gonna keep quiet and go with the flow I don't want them thinking that they know me and I am not staying here that's for sure, I want to be with my boys. Sue goes on about the home, the rules and my dietary needs. I say I have none and will eat whatever, but I don't like vegetables or Honey Nut Loops cereal. I get introduced to the others that live here.

Sue introduces me to Sam.

"Sam this is Mo. He is staying with us now."

Sam is a girl who you would consider a boy at first glance. She has short blond hair, boyish looks and wears Nike 110 trainers (nice ones as well), a Nike t-shirt and tracky bottoms. I notice she has got loads of slash marks on her arms and a tattoo on her wrist that says nanna.

She looks at me all stone-faced and says, "Hello," followed by, "what are you? Are you Pakistani or something? I have never seen an Asian kid in care before."

Sue cuts in and says something about it not being any of her business, the thing is she wasn't being racist she just wanted to know. I don't answer her question I just nod my head up and say alright.

Paul comes down next and says, "Alright," and is straight out of the door, he smokes weed I can tell straight away.

In the dining room is a young lad about 10 or 11 called Ben and another young kid called Emma They are both being home schooled by a teacher who looks like he is about to give up on life. I get introduced and we go back into the office upstairs.

"There is also another girl who stays here called Jody; she is missing from home at the minute."

I watch closely to where Sue gets the money from. There is a safe under the desk and the key to it is on a bunch which says duty keys; she signs the sheet to say she has taken the money, locks the safe and puts the keys on a hook on the far side of the room!

As we go out it starts to hail stone, the weather is mad at the minute. One second it's sunny the next it's freezing. One thing we always can talk about on the camps is the weather. The thing is with Manchester is, if you don't like the weather, hang around for five minutes, it will change. Vinnie says this all the time I think it's funny and true. We gets to Sues car, it's a really smart Audi A3 the same as my mate has who I used to get weed off, only this one has all leather interior and is a 2.0 litre engine. Sue lets me get in the front, officially we are supposed to get in the back of the car when we are with a care worker it is something to do with protecting the worker or something, someone once explained but I was not listening.

During the drive there Sue has a CD on playing some music which is crap. She is humming the song and occasionally a couple of words from the chorus. I think it is Beyoncé. Whatever it is I don't like it. I think she notices this and puts Capital Radio on low then starts asking me questions about where I have been and stuff.

"How come you have been staying in the homeless camps, Mo; did you not like the home in Wigan?"

"Yeah," I answer but say nothing else.

"Have read in your reports that you have been using NEW PSYCOACTIVE SUBSTANCES?"

"What's that?" I say.

"I think they call them legal highs, like spice and other substances?"

"Oh right," I say and nothing more. She is getting nothing from me; I have half a joint in my pocket and a bag of spice gold too. I will be smoking the joint in the toilet the second we get out of this car.

We get to the Trafford Centre and park on the top floor. I tell Sue I need the toilet, and will meet her outside Foot Locker, she says it is not a problem and walks with me to the toilet as it is on the way. I light the joint and smoke it fast. When I get out toilet the high it hits me, I feel good, but tired and at the same time my stomach cramp has gone.

"Where did you say you wanted to go, Mo? Foot Locker?"

"Yeah," I say with a smile on my face I cannot get off. "Do you like your job, Sue? How long have you worked here?"

"I have worked in residential care for 10 years, before that I was a teaching assistant."

"Oh right. Can we go to JD sports after Foot Locker for a track suit?"

"Yes, do you know what ones you want?"

"I want the huaraches or the 110s that Sam had."

We get the clothes and I wear the tracky and trainers straight away, we also get some underwear and socks I even get a small Nike bag to go over my shoulder. Then we go to a nice restaurant called Frankie and Benny's. I like Sue... But I'm not staying.

23

The Funeral

Vinnie

I cannot believe the turn out for my dad's funeral. It's a top turn out. There are people from Broughton and Cheetham Hill and even a couple of school friends. Fifty-eight is an awful age to die or should I fucking say murdered by the council bastards. It took two weeks to release his body as there was a toxicology report to be done. I was even taken in for fucking questioning as well from the fucking coppers! I kicked off big time in the station and was charged with assaulting a police officer, but it was thankfully dropped. I am not gonna be dropping the case against the council though, the bastards! I have called Saul and the solicitors can take it from here. I have a claim in too.

The official cause of his death is carbon monoxide poisoning, this explains me crashing out on the couch all the time and sleeping heavily. I always liked the window open in the flat as I like the breeze and sound of the weather to send me to sleep. If I did not do this I would have probably have been dead too. It's the only thing I like about sleeping in the tent; the clean air, the wind and the noise it makes me feel alive. Unlike my FUCKING DAD! Calm down, Vin calm down. I let the pall bearers carry his coffin and me and my sister just follow behind with her two kids in tow. That slag would not let me see my girls or bring them to his funeral.

My dad's service is short and the priest says some words on my behalf. I would only get upset if I started talking. It dawns on me during his eulogy that I am now an orphan, which makes me chuckle on the inside as I think I might go to Barnardo's with George when he ever gets out.

We did not have much money for the funeral. My sister put a Facebook page up and people donated some money to the cost and the buffet. After the service we went to a social club, it wasn't a local of his and it was quite far from where we live, but all the pubs have closed down on our estate where he lived and the estate he grew up on are now posh flats and the houses and pubs are gone long ago. None of the lads from the camps are here, which I am glad of, to be honest, as a few of the lads here would flare their nostrils at the group I am with at the minute. It's a joke because we are all from the same shitty council estates, but the minute anyone earns a few quid from grafting drugs and opens a "beauty salon" for their moll they think they are royalty! I mean let's be honest, driving a one year old Golf GTI or a Merc 180 does not make you all middle class and enable to live in a Cheshire postcode. The way I see it, you will get nicked sooner or later like I did and have to do your sentence and STILL HAVE TO PAY A FUCKING DEBT WHEN YOU GET OUT. So fuck 'em, let them have their five minutes of fame.

Macca comes over to me with his absolute darling of a bird; she's probably about 16 or 17 and pregnant to him. That's her fucked for life, yet she thinks she just got a meal ticket for life!!

"Alright, Vinnie, sorry to hear about your dad pal, he was a good bloke when we was growing up he would even have a kick about on the green with us."

"Thanks, Macca. I really appreciate you coming today pal, all the lads have shown up and it really has surprised me. I owe money to couple of 'em here as well," I laugh.

Macca introduces Toni to me who just smiles and puts her head to the floor. Fuck me, I think Macca has got this one trained from the get go she is right in her place. You see people like Macca (and me if I am honest) can see vulnerable people and damaged goods a mile away, it's in our genes. He simply plays the caring hand until she is under his spell then gives her a wakeup call she has probably seen before to her mum or by her previous boyfriend. Macca once said to me and I quote "It really gets on my nerves when a girl I am seeing tries to play me off with that 'my ex-boyfriend is a bastard, he used to hit me card' I go quiet for a second and drop it on her like... Oh really, what for? I mean it could not have been for nothing, he is not just gonna come in and start slapping you up for nothing, you MUST have done something?" He says they look at him in shock at first then laugh it off like he was joking, but they soon find out!

"Well, it is good to see you pal, sorry it is at your dad's funeral like, if any good comes out of it at least you did not go too and you should be looking at a few quid compo; I know you would rather still have your dad here though."

"I know, mate but what can I do now? We are all devastated," I lie.

Macca gets me a beer and I go outside with it for a joint. I really need to stop smoking Spice; it's becoming a daily habit since he died.

24

Banged Up

George

Some prick has nicked my fucking brew flask and I am gonna smash him when I see him. I have been sentenced to four months on top of what I have done previously, meaning I am out of here at the end of July. I got two weeks solitary and two weeks added to my sentence for the parcel and it was dealt with in here by the governor. I am allowed to share a cell with some lad from Moss Side. He is proper heavy and is looking at ten years, but he has it sorted on the outside. He is the same age as me and was driving about in a new BMW X5, the house he had got raided and his prints was on the gun and bullets as well as being found with a weed grow in the house and half a kilo of cocaine. He was trying to say the drugs are not his but the house they were renting was in his name. Hussain (Sane) has a parcel being thrown over today and I will collect it in the yard and carry it back through.

"When you are in the yard, my bro will call the lad from the pad. Just hang about, okay bro?"

"Safe bro. What they dropping?" George says, but really does not care, he just wants to make conversation.

"Two phones, some brown, weed and spice, it will be compressed as usual so you will have no problem plugging it all, bro." Sane speaks to George with some respect at this point. He is just a pawn in the game and will be used and sacrificed at Sane's needs. He thinks to himself that this lad is so thick he could probably get him to plead guilty to his charges. The thing is he has his uses at the minute and will give him a false sense of security on the wing until he is surplus to requirements.

The Screw unlocks the pad door and I go out with Sane on to the landing, nobody is taking the piss at the minute as they know that me and sane will smash 'em. Obviously I stick up for my boys and he has my back too.

We get out to the yard, it is pissing down but obviously I am not arsed about that I need the gear as half of the spice is mine. I walk over to the yard and I reckon that Sane's boy on the other wing is looking in to the yard on his phone. The parcel drops, *thud* into the grass, I don't even look around I just pick it up and store it under my top. *Thud* another one drops. A lad picks it up and walks over to the fucking screws. What a prick. The gear is in a Kinder Egg toy container and the phones are taped together. I will have to plug it now and leave the paper in the yard as these fuckers are gonna check us all. I walk behind two lads who are talking.

"Just stay there lads one second."

They do not answer, they just ignore me as they know what the score is. I can see the screw on his radio we are all going back in and getting patted down. I push the egg up first and have to put the phones together which scrapes me as they go in. I clench myself and can feel them being sucked into me. I walk in on my own and get patted down and go through with no issues. Obviously the prick who handed the parcel in is fucking dead no two ways about it. An eighth of spice cost £20 on the outside, in some UK prisons the price of an eighth sells upwards of £100.00.

25

Business

Ricky

I have been doing alright with the spice selling. Jazz is like a mate now I can see he is happy, he even gave me a mobile phone the other day and said that it would be easy for people to contact me for spice. I smashed mine arguing with Janey the other night. My hands are healing well but they are still sore so I am constantly smoking spice to ease the pain. Mo has not been on the camp for a week now. Vinnie has his flat but still stays down here a couple of nights a week and George is still inside, I hear he will be out near August.

I currently have Naomi, Joel, Louis, Jody, Gregg, Preston, Kane, Joe, Jarek and the Polish lot all buying from me on camp. There is also another camp on Oxford Road where all the squatters from the bank are staying. A guy was selling on there for Jazz but I hear he has fucked off to Blackpool so they are all coming to me. I said to Janey that I bet around £150 a day comes to me just from the begging on the streets. Preston spends £25 every day and he gets it from begging outside the cash machine in Piccadilly Gardens. He was even complaining the other day that everyone wants to feed him, he does not mind the coffees, but there is only so much Greggs and Boots sandwiches you can eat in a day, he just wants the money for fuck's sake.

My problem is that I am smoking all the time and Janey says I have a twitch in my face. Both our stomachs are bad, but everyone's is and I get like a bone ache which is hard to explain.

We are earning money and one night we stayed in a bed and breakfast for the night and I left the spice with Joel who is a good lad really. Other than that I haven't really moved from the camp for a good couple of weeks now other than go to Elysium which is where I am off now.

I walk in and I can hear Jazz saying something in Urdu to the two lads that are working with him. I automatically feel he is slagging me off as I detect a smirk from one of the lads. Jazz is a good guy but I will give it to him if I think he is taking the piss out of me in his language.

"Ricky, how are you bro, have you got my money?"

"Safe pal, yeah your money is here, is that your new car on the front?"

"Yes it is, do you like it?"

"Fuck me, Jazz you must be earning some money in here?"

"No bro, I have leased it £280 a month. You need to work 16 hour days like us and you can have these things."

I quickly hit back, "What's the sense of working so hard if you never have anytime to have fun?" As I say it

I realise I work twenty-four hours selling this shit for this twat!

Jazz realises the same thing and says, "Each to their own, Ricky, each to their own," and changes the subject, as he knows that explaining business to this smelly junkie is pointless. He is just happy that he has survived so long and keeps coming in with the money.

"Where's Janey? Are you still together?"

"Yeah she is okay, she is in the camp." Jazz would love to tell him that his mates have both had sex with Janey and it cost them £15 each when she was whoring off the back of Sackville Street a few months ago. They recognised her when she came in the shop one day, the thing is she did not even recognise them or she let on that she didn't. Jazz thinks he will save that atom bombshell for a rainy day and hopefully she may come in one day on her own and he will get her in the back with him.

"I still have a bit left from the other day, but I will have the four ounce and come back when it has gone is that okay?"

Jazz sighs like he is doing ME the favour and nods in agreement. The deal is done and I leave the shop after building a joint. When I get outside I see Dermo coming across the road.

"Easy Dermo, how are bro?"

Dermo looks at Ricky up and down and lets on back, "Alright Ricky, you still smoking that spice, pal? You're not looking too good, pal. Seems to have a grip on you, I told you, you would be better on the brown. Do you want any?"

My insides want to tell him to fuck right off, but I cannot be bothered and I haven't got much of a fight in me now I ignore him and carry on walking. I just want to get back, I really don't like the way people are treating me like some homeless scruff! I might be living amongst 'em but I AM NOT LIKE THEM. I am not sure if I am paranoid but people don't look at me any more when I am walking towards them and I swear a woman has just held on to her bag as I was approaching her, what the fuck does she think I am? Do I look like a low-life smack head bag snatcher or something? This day is horrible, I just want back in my tent where it is peaceful and none of the stress is around me. I really need to get back.

Ricky can feel his heart beating faster and he has a feeling of panic, anxiety and with tightness across his chest. He thinks he is having a heart attack, little does he realise that this is his first panic attack which will slowly take away his confidence and steal the remainder of his social skills. This really is the beginning of a bad road for him, in some ways it is worse than the heart attack he thought he was having, as the mental torture he will now have to endure will stay with him... until he gives up spice that is.

I get back in the tent and open a can of coke and drink it in one. I am sweating really badly again it's pouring off me. I relight the joint and take a big drag and lie back. The spice reacts with my body and mind I begin to relax and come round with Janey nudging me.

"Hey, give me some of that I must have passed out again. This gear is so strong, but it really does make me feel so fucking amazing."

I take my top off to change into the other t-shirt as it is soaking wet.

"Mr Skinny," Janey says smiling. "I wish I was that skinny."

No one has ever called me skinny, ever. I must have lost some weight since Christmas; wonder what I weigh, I remember being 12 stone 10 oz in the doctors in December I weighed myself when he was pissing about on the computer printing my script off.

"I'm not skinny, I'm ripped," I say back to her.

Janey laughs again and says, "Have you looked at your face? You look chiselled like a super model, you're skin and bone."

I have not looked at my face for ages when I think about it. I have nothing to say back to her I take a drag of the joint then, get on top of her.

26

Mo Money Mo Problems

Mo

I have stayed here for over a week; it's been okay, but it is time to get off to see the boys now I speak with Jim who is on shift.

"Hiya Jim, can I have my spends, please?"

Jim is a young worker who is still in his first twelve months, he thinks he can save us all and is still working on the vibe of things happening to him first time round. Like when Emma threw a glass of milk in his face the other morning because he asked if she was going into school today, "fuck off paedo" then she just chucked at him. That was his naivety. An experienced worker would just say hello or good morning and leave her be. But like I said to him, there's no point crying over spilt milk.

"Hi Mo, you can have your spends later, we don't give them out in school hours so it will be after five p.m. What takeaway would you like tonight for tea?"

"I'm not sure," I say to him. I have no plans to be here then. The only good thing to come out of this week is the lad at the corner shop is covering the shop for his

93

uncle while he is on holiday and he is selling me spice on the quiet, so it has been quite easy for me so far. I have been told about smoking in my room, they think it is a cig because they cannot recognise the smell yet. Sue let me off with sanctioning my spends as she said she did not want to start off on a bad foot.

Emma and Ben are outside with Nigel cleaning the mini bus. We cannot officially do any labour in the house as it is against the UNICEF or Save the Children laws or something, anyway we can ask to help clean or paint but we cannot be forced to labour. I have folded some post it notes I took from Jim before and put it between the bottom of the hinge side of door and the jamb. I am hoping that when Jim leaves the office it will look like the door has closed, but still be ajar a bit and not locked. This is a trick George taught me and he said it works if the door is held open by a wedge and has a door closer fitted. Once the wedge is removed the door will automatically close to the lock, but the folded paper should just keep it slightly open.

"Jim, I think Ben wants you, mate." I say this as I am walking into my room.

"Thanks, Mo." Ben stands up and leaves the office with the door closing behind him. As I hear him go down the stairs I walk into the office then take the duty keys off the hook, open the safe and take out the petty cash safe. I lock the safe put the keys back and go into my room, taking the post it note away from the bottom of the door leaving the office locked. I think I have just committed the perfect crime. I feel the adrenaline hit me and I need the toilet, but I have to play cool. I put my coat on and go outside with an old rucksack on my back. I walk out the door and Ben and Jim shout me to them.

"Where you off to, Mo?" shouts Ben.

I just look at them and keep walking away and mumble to my mates. I light my joint; I can feel their eyes on me as I am walking down the street with a rucksack on my back and petty cash till inside. I am feeling really good but I MUST go to the toilet quick… spice, I'm sure it messes your stomach up.

The cash tin is locked and I don't have a screwdriver to open it. I use another option to force it open. I leave the cash tin in the rucksack, twist it so the tin cannot move and smash it repeatedly against the wall until I hear it break. It breaks in about seven hits and the monies are all in the bag. I made the mistake once of throwing the cash tin against the wall and the coins went everywhere, leaving me to pick it all up. There is £85 in cash and £11.40 in coins I am well happy, time to go see the boys in the camps.

I get to the camps around two p.m. Ricky is here with Janey, Vinnie has shown up and looks in a bad way Kane, Preston, Joe, Louis and Naomi are in a bad way too they look like they have been up for a few days straight.

"Check you all smart," says Vinnie who notices Mo is sporting his style.

"Hiya Vinnie, you alright?"

"Yes pal, buzzing," Ricky nods at me and I notice that his bandages are off and he has scratches on the side of his face. Then Janey comes out and she has a big lump around her eye. It looks like they have been at it with each other.

"What's happening Mo, thought you had left us pal?"

"They moved me to a house in Wythenshawe, innit."

A girl pops her head out of the tent and says, "Do you live in Clapham house in Wythenshawe?"

"Yeah," I reply.

"That's my fucking house too."

"Did they mention me? I'm Jody."

"Sue just said you lived there but was not there at the minute."

"Don't tell 'em you have seen me okay, especially that slag Sue, I fucking hate her, the bitch."

I say no more and go round the alley to have a pee, it smells bad and I think someone has been shitting around here too.

27

Love and Hate

Janey

I've had no sleep and I need sleep. It sets off my anxiety and my depression. I need sleep. He thinks I sleep all the time but I don't I get a few hours here and there. I know I look bad and I cannot face leaving the tent at the minute, especially as it is getting lighter now. I don't want anyone to see me, ANYONE! I see a girl who works in the town hall nearly every day going past me. I did not know where I knew her face from, but it clicked she used to be in a school I went to for a few months. We used to laugh at her and call her because she had ginger hair and loads of freckles. She is gorgeous now. She is all done up nice and her skin is beautiful. She wears high heeled shoes and a matching skirt with her jacket. I Saw her smile one morning when she was chatting to a business guy holding a Starbucks coffee Her teeth was pure white against her what I can only guess to be an expensive designer lipstick. I noticed she looked at me then quickly looked away when our eyes met. My teeth are rotting away from the sides, I don't brush them anymore and we have stopped buying the baby wipes to wash with. Prior to that we could get showers at the YPSF but we have not been there in ages too, I just can't face anyone. I know I am in a bad way and I think that's why I did what I did to him.

We had been drinking all day and smoking spice, the two don't mix and I don't mix well with alcohol especially vodka. Louis is back on the camps, his mam has kicked him out again and he went on the rob in Tesco and came back with 3 litres of vodka. Ricky was saying to me that we are good together and he has fell for me, I thought this was really nice and for once I felt good about myself. He was then asking me about me exes and about Nate. He was really jealous. I tried reassuring him that he was the best I have been with and I love him, but the nicer I was to him the more angry he got. He then started to call me a slag and comparing me to a girl he still loves called Leah and I am nothing like her I am just a scruffy slag. By this time we were screaming at each other. I dug my nails right into his face and neck and scrapped them all down and then I lost it AGAIN! I started to scream and kick over the tents I remember screaming about not being able to sleep. Ricky said he was going to kill me I ran at him and he hit me with the bottle above my eye. I am not sure how long I was knocked out for, but there was quite a bit of blood in the tent when I got up. He was not there I don't know where he went, but in the morning when he come back he said he was sorry and begged me not to go to the hospital as could get him put away again. I said I would not and we made up. Don't think for a second I am letting him win this one. I will abide my time and exact my revenge at his lowest point. He thinks he is better than all of us in the camps and he thinks that his story is different to everyone else, he is a waster I can see that now, his good looks and his dominance is coming to an end in this camp, he is the only one who does not see it. Right now I need him for his money and spice, I need this space but when I am ready I am off again just like last time.

Part 2

1

The Professionals' Conference. 15/05/15

Chairperson: Julie Renn CEO Life Share Manchester.

Minutes from Manchester City Council's youth service recorded by Samina Begum, MCCYS.

Apologies: Dept. Governor Mike Phipps, HMP Manchester. Claire Summers, Addiction dependency Service MCR.

Attendees: Jennifer Williams, Manchester Evening News, John Murphy, ADS Manchester, Steve Jones, YPSF Manchester, Daniel Goodyear, Safe Stay Manchester, Jay Smith, Elizabeth House MCR, Tom White, GMYN (Greater Manchester Youth Network), Pat Kearney, Manchester City Council, Chief Constable Malcom Braithwaite, GMP, John Cloud, NW ambulance service.

Agenda:

1. Number of homeless young people in the city 16-24 using NPS (new psychoactive substance) in the city

2. Strategy to support and reduce harm of young homeless people in Manchester

3. Source private funders to finance two outreach youth workers to provide a six month study into the side effects of spice and the average spend a day and to engage daily in the camps and build intense relationships

4. Housing all homeless in the city

5. Build a working relationship with Elysium Manchester

6. Securing Brazennose Street archway removing homeless people

7. People refusing to go to work when in supported accommodation

8. Collective response to the report from recent national data doc. (below)

Steve Jones begins stating there are thirty-seven homeless people on the street aged between 18-24 and six 15-17 year olds. This is recorded by his outreach team who have refused to adhere to the council's policy that only people that are actually "sat down" on the floor under shelter can be counted as homeless. Councillor Kearney challenges this and states the actual stats are 17 from their outreach team. Steve Jones challenges back because the council will do their data at three p.m. on a Friday afternoon when the young people are active in the city and this is a conflicting report to show a positive outcome for the city.

John cloud speaks of harm reduction and believes the intravenous drug users and alcohol users are at high risk and the NPS users of spice are at low risk of death as the factual stats on heart attacks cannot be conclusive as there are not government stats to support or defend the alleged statistics of the NHS. John Cloud request for MCC to request urgent funds for a detox centre to be pushed as soon as possible to reduce actual bodily harm being self-inflicted to spice and other NPS users in the homeless camps.

Pat Kearney confirmed that Brantwood (Manchester Development Company and philanthropist) will pay for two outreach youth workers on a twelve month fixed contract with the council overseeing the employment contract.

Daniel Goodyear and Jay Smith state that there are 14 empty spaces in the youth hostels in Manchester right now and even if we had fifty places due to Manchester CC policy on rent arrears the young people on the street could not be housed as all are in some form of debt with the hostels and those that have never been in supported accommodation have not completed the council's mandatory house training course and will remain at band 5 and are considered Not PRIORITY so therefore will not be housed. Pat Kearney stands by this and the policy will not be changed.

Pat Kearney states that Brazen nose street arch way will have two 12 foot steel fences erected and Either side of the archway to prevent the homeless returning once the enforcement officers remove them on May 23rd this is challenged by all who again protest that the council are just moving the problem and not fixing it. PK responds in the defence of the local businesses that have been affected in the last six months due to the chaos and intimidation created by the camp.

YP in the youth hostels will not go into work due to cost of rent once in employment and living in a youth hostel. Currently £249.00 per week Pat Kearney has agreed to work with ALL the hostels and will pay the housing benefits for six months for any person in employment whilst living the hostels with the support from the Hostel staff and supporting agencies that they will be moved on to their own accommodation after. This is a surprise from the council which is supported by all in the room.

PLEASE SEE DOC BELOW REGARDING THE FINAL MINUTES OF THE MEETING.

Next meeting is set for 1/09/16

Samina Begum

Case study into the effects of smoking Cannabinoids, AKA spice

Background: The market for synthetic cannabinoid smoking mixtures called 'spice',

'Synthetic cannabis' (or 'noids') is well established, although UK prevalence is still largely unknown.

The vast majority of the market is made up of pre-packaged branded products. These branded products contain a non-psychoactive dried plant base that has been dipped or sprayed with one or more of a range of synthetic cannabinoids. Some of these products are marketed as 'ultra-potent'.

There are numerous media reports of Accident and Emergency admissions caused by synthetic cannabinoid mixtures. Although there are no available statistics these reports often involve brands such as Spice gold Black Mamba *Clockwork Orange, Sensate, Pandora's Box* etc.

that are known to be highly potent and all termed as Spice!

Recent media reports have associated two products with the brand names *Psyclone* and *Exodus Damnation* with causing a heart attack and the deaths of two people in the UK There is no confirmation these products caused these deaths as media reports are frequently inaccurate.

However, both of these products contain a blend of two synthetic cannabinoids, 5F-AKB48 and 5F-PB228 and both are reportedly highly potent.

Brand: This information briefing looks at what is known about potent brands of synthetic cannabinoid smoking mixtures, focusing on two current brands *Psyclone* and *Exodus Damnation and the newest addition Annihilation 44*

Physical effects: The physical effects of the more potent brands can be quite overpowering with reports of breathing difficulties, tight chest, racing heart, palpitations, shakes and sweats which can lead to severe panic. With higher doses balance and psychomotor skills can be severely impaired. Loss of feeling and numbness in limbs, nausea/vomiting, collapse and unconsciousness has also been reported. The eyes take on cannabis-like pink colour or a zombie like blood shot red. Sudden skin rashes have also been reported.

Risks and harms: Harms associated with synthetic cannabinoids are well documented and include:

- Agitation,
- Seizures,
- Hypertension,
- Emesis (vomiting)
- Hypokalaemia (low potassium levels).
- Epileptic seizures
- Collapse/unconsciousness
- Anaphylactic shock
- Inability to move limbs
- Paranoia
- Symptoms similar to that of psychosis
- Anxiety/fear
- Increased levels of aggression
- Low mood

Although some of these symptoms are similar to high doses of cannabis, researchers have concluded that synthetic cannabinoids are potentially more harmful than cannabis.

As with natural cannabis, synthetic cannabinoids are associated with triggering psychotic symptoms in those predisposed to the illness. Whether the more potent pre-packaged synthetic cannabinoid mixtures are more likely to adversely affect mental health is unknown.

Tolerance to synthetic cannabinoids develops quickly, with increasing dosage and compulsive use commonly reported. It is not thought that synthetic cannabinoids produce physical dependence, but like natural cannabis some people may become anxious about stopping and originally many experienced mild withdrawal symptoms, such as sweating, insomnia and vivid dreams. It is reported these symptoms generally subside between 7-14 days, however withdrawals according to recent users and some prison wardens have said the withdrawals can last up to twenty days and give severe pains, ache sweats and flu-like symptoms.

There is also some evidence that links synthetic cannabinoid use with acute kidney injury as well as loss of bowel controls and stiff aching bones. Further to this it is reported in the health clinics and by young female users that they believe Spice is a form of contraception, as most of the young women are still having their monthly cycles, yet none of them are being caught pregnant and all are sexually active. Another response to this is that it may be the males that are infertile from the spice use and not the women. These notes cannot be carried out as conclusive as there have been no recorded fertility tests on any NPS dependent users.

2

Out On Tag

George

My solicitor has put in for me to be released on a tag if
Lee can guarantee that I have a fixed abode, which is
looking like Safe Stay. Obviously I will be on a seven
a.m. to seven p.m. curfew for the remainder of my
sentence, but I am not arsed I want out of here now and
will stay there until my sentence is over. I want that
prick Lee to sort me out with a flat as well. The funny
thing is that Louis from our camp has just been sent
down for none payment of fines. I saw him in here the
other day, he says everyone is okay, Ricky is earning
money, Janey is still a daft bitch and Vinnie is smoking
and drinking a lot of spice since his dad died. Mo is back
on the camp, but they are all getting moved as the
council have put a notice up on the camp saying the
bailiffs will remove them this week. He is funny Louis
and does not give a fuck apparently the magistrate said
he would be forced to send him to jail if he did not
comply, Louis told me.

He said, "look, I am not on benefits and I am
homeless I cannot pay my fines and probably will never

get out of debt with them, so just send me to prison and I can start again clean."

The magistrate thought he was taking the piss at first, then had pity and give him nine weeks.

Sane is no longer with me he got 10 years and shipped out to another nick. He left me some gear and trainers as an apology for smacking me up last week. I told the screw I fell off the bed, I am not arsed really Sane is a safe guy and he said that he will hook me up with his boys when he is out one day. The thing is with Sane he spoke too much on that phone and I know where his secret stash is.

I am now padded with a guy who is from Liverpool, not too far from where I am from, he likes smoking heroin, but has just started smoking spice. When he had his first joint he was stuck to the cell wall for an hour, says it was one of the best hits he has ever had. The lad loves it as much as me.

3

Cheeky Bastards

Vinnie

The fucking council have not only stopped my housing benefit because I did not get my doctor's note, they have also put a notice up on the camp to remove us. A specky cunt in a suit came the other day giving us one week's notice. He also brought two security guys with him for protection. At first I was fuming because I had just got kicked out of Elizabeth House for an argument with another lad. I smashed him up and down the hall way and it was on camera. I was given a twenty-four hour notice and had to go. FUCKERS! I had another fight the other night with some lads from London, they had been clubbing in at Panacea and thought it would be funny to come in the tents filming on their phones and putting it on YouTube. BIG FUCKING MISTAKE. I smashed fuck out of the biggest of their crew with Ricky and little Mo even tried gouging the eyes out of one of them. The Polish lads started laying into them as well; Patrik is one sick fuck, he completely lost it. They were on their phones shouting "bring the gun down" to someone and all that bollocks, but I knew no nob heads from down

111

south would be strap. There are probably five lads in Manchester now who are crazy enough to just shoot someone from a fight and those pricks was not in that bracket. The next time they want to humiliate someone who is in their lowest ebb I think they will think twice. People think because we are homeless we will not fight or stand up for ourselves. The way I see it, us homeless people have got fuck all to lose, we are dangerous people and most of us have drug, alcohol and mental health issues. We don't live in the same society or by the same rules as Joe Public.

Anyway, we kind of had a meeting and decided that we were not going to go to Oxford Road camp. It's a big camp and with the weather getting better and it is lighter for longer there is a good vibe there. It's like the festival season has started. The public are dropping off clothes, food and even money. The leftist groups are staging protest in support of our rights but the issue is you are being monitored by every one of the council's homeless agencies there and we don't want that, plus Ricky does not want to be sleeping where he is supplying to. I am also in with a cut of the profits too so we don't want to fuck it up for ourselves. Joe has found us a place at the bottom of Deansgate next to the metro which is sheltered and a really good spot. So we are picking up camp in the morning and getting away from this shit hole.

4

Engagement

Lee

I have been tasked by Spencer, my line manager, to get Janey, Ricky, George (upon release) all back engaging with the programme.

"The issue I have, Spencer is that they are all hooked on the spice and do not want anything to do with me until they are in absolute crisis."

"I do understand, Lee, but we are a target-driven programme and paid by results, as you know since the cuts things have changed dramatically." Spencer has worked with homeless people for 25 years and has been up and down the management ladder many times."

At no point in Lee's career has he ever met someone who has in-depth knowledge of social and housing policy whilst still maintaining a connection with the street homeless people. Lee has the upmost respect for Spencer, but is frustrated on the task he has been given. Lee's target is to get 50% of his clients into accommodation and in full or part-time employment in the next year.

"I will try to get them all out for breakfast once a week to start and build from there. I did speak with Janey last week, she says that Ricky is being very abusive to her in the recent months and the relationship is becoming more violent, he even slashed the tent while she was in it with rage. I have informed her that the minute she wants out to let me know and we can refer her to a domestic violence support shelter. The bonus to this for her is there is no red tape blocking her because of her rent arrears."

"That sounds like a good plan, Lee. You can also pick a few pay as you go phones from Tesco if you like to give to them. As an incentive, there is money in the funds to go to Blackpool Pleasure Beach – can you see if they will come?"

Lee finishes off his supervision with Spencer, all is good with regards to progressing with his other ten clients; four are into work and have their own accommodation in Rochdale and Oldham Boroughs, but none are in accommodation in Manchester and are still classed as "sofa surfing".

Lee puts on his North Face jacket, his rucksack on his back and with his expensive Nike trainers; he stands out as a youth worker like a sore thumb. Youth workers, especially outreach workers always carry a rucksack for their documents and sundries. They wear expensive comfortable trainers and have a quality wind and waterproof jacket. This keeps them warm and dry in a city as wet and dry as Manchester, plus when the weather changes (frequently) they can fold the jacket and pop it into the rucksack. The clothes they opt for are also a good way of breaking the barrier with the young people as young people love good trainers. It is always a topic for discussion about the latest new edition of Nike and Adidas and the youth workers do not look like an authoritarian figure that has been a negative presence in their lives for many years. My task now is to find them. Lee realises that they have probably moved, he decides to speak with the outreach team from YPSF to see if they have any update on where they have moved to.

5

Clearer Skies

George

I have my release papers and cannot wait to go. There are six with me this morning getting out, a couple of the lads have been in for over 10 years and apart from the odd day release they have not had to be on the outside alone. I can see they are buzzing, but one of the lads looks scared. He has no family like me and has spent nearly my lifetime inside for different offences. I think it is mad how a bloke like him can be dead confident in here but unsure out there. I am sure he will be okay in a few days it; obviously will take a week or so to adapt, innit.

I walk out on to the road and can see Lee's Ford Focus with the shit alloys, he thinks he is the main man with that car, but I would never be seen driving that, no way. I walk across to him and say hello and get in the car.

"How are you, George, are you okay?"

"Yeah, sound am I going to Safe Stay?"

"Yes, there is a G4S officer coming at six p.m. to put your tag on. You will be on a seven a.m. to seven p.m.

curfew and have to attend probation appointments three times a week as part of your bail conditions."

I say nothing to him, we will see how it goes with the tag but obviously I am not gonna stay in every night for three months am I? What do they think I am? Lee goes on about some Prince's Trust course he wants me to go on next week.

"I have done loads of them shit courses before. Even been on holiday with them and stuff. I have my first aid qualification, I have level 1 on plastering, plumbing and have also done food safety courses and all sorts of other shit what do I need this for?"

"George, listen to me pal. I feel you are in a real difficult part in your life. I am also going to refer you to Addiction Dependency service, is this okay?"

"I won't go," George replies instantly.

"Why not, pal? Can you tell me why you would not just visit the ADS?"

"I don't have a problem, I am alright. I like doing what I do, I don't really drink, all I do is smoke spice and have a bit of Charlie if it's there. I won't buy it."

Lee does not push the topic further, he feels the lad has had a hard few months, hard life to be honest and drops the conversation.

"Do you want anything to eat? Would you like a kebab or anything?"

"Yeah, a pizza and a coke, can you go to the one just here."

When they pull over, Lee realises it is 20 metres away from Elysium.

"Can you go in for it, mate? I will have a ciggie outside the shop."

117

"Yes sure. Do you just want a regular cheese and tomato?"

"Yeah."

Lee comes out of the shop and cannot see George. He looks down the street and can see him with a group of five young men outside of the "smoking" shop known as Elysium. He curses himself as he should have known what George's plans were when he pulled up. Protocol says he is not officially allowed to approach, as Lee is potentially putting himself at risk, but he decides to drive up to them. Lee pulls over and the window winds down on the passenger side.

"George, I have got your stuff here pal."

George is smoking what lee assumes to be a joint of Spice.

"I'm alright," says George.

"Are you getting in?"

One of the lads shouts to George so Lee can hear, "Tell your pal to fuck off, George."

Lee calls to him once more and reminds him of his six p.m. appointment. George responds back to him, "Yeah, in a bit" and laughs with the lads.

For the first time in his fifteen-year career as a youth worker he feels like his pride has been hurt and he has been treated as a mug. This does not usually bother him as he knows how the stories end, but today when he drives off he hears himself say, "Fuck the scruffy twat." He calms himself down and enjoys the pizza and coke and feels he is losing the ability to care and needs a new job. One where you actually see some rewards!

6

Back Home

Mo

I am feeling really poorly, I want my mum and my family. I am shivering and have the runs really bad. I feel dead hot and cold too. I cannot go back home through all that has happened, but I can go to the care home. I need a bed and to rest. I don't say anything to anyone as I go. Jody is outside the tent.

"You okay, Mo? You look pale, mate."

"Hmm, yeah I'm okay?" I walk off the camp and head to the tram stop.

The bonus to moving from Brazennose Street to here is we are directly under the Metrolink and it takes two minutes to get to the tram stop. It's early morning and the commuters are getting off the tram on the other side of the track on their way to work. I am slouched on the seating area looking at the sign that states there are "3 mins" to the next tram. Hurry up, I need to get to the home. I have not felt like this since I was a young kid when I had the bad fever when I came back from my dad's family home in Pakistan. I loved it there; the village was so beautiful and calm. The people were so

119

nice. We played cricket all the time and it was so much easier than living in England, no hustle bustle, no long school hours just relaxing in the village and my gran would cook for us every night. We visited cousins and friends and even went into the city. I would like to go back one day but right now I just want a bed.

Yesterday was my sixteenth birthday and I felt great. I had plenty of spice and Janey bought me a Krunchy Fried Chicken take away for my birthday, the weather was good and the vibe on the camp was okay. Today is a different world, I so wish I could go to my mum for one night.

Mo realises he is crying as he feels the tears run down his cheeks, he wonders why he cannot be normal like all the other kids. Like the ones on his street or the ones in his old school. He was always treated differently by his mum and his dad never gave him much time, not the same time he gave to his younger brother and two elder sisters. Mo knew it was because he was never any good at school. He has problems sitting in the class room he struggles reading and he just does not understand the things the teacher in his small class explains to him. He was diagnosed with Attention Deficit Disorder when he was just nine years old. He remembers his dad being upset and kind of angry; his mum was relieved as they at least had answers to his behaviour pattern.

Mo can feel himself getting weaker, he feels like he is going to be sick. The motion of the tram is really nauseating. As the tram stops he stands up and vomits the remaining contents of his stomach into the carriage. He leaves the tram and heads to the house. The house is only five minutes away from where he gets off. He walks along the road with his hands in his tracksuit pockets, his shoulders are pushing into his neck, this is an attempt to stop the rain from dropping onto his neck. The wind is blowing it in his direction and each cold rain drop that hits his neck is making him feel weaker. A white car pulls up alongside him. It's Sue. She gets out of the car.

"Mo, are you okay?"

Mo shakes his head at her;

Sue gets out of the car and walks round to the pavement, puts her arm around Mo and slowly escorts him into the car. Sue comforts him like a mum, her voice is soft and caring, she reassures him that he is ok and she will have him rested in his bed as soon as he get in.

"How did you know it was me?"

"I bought you the clothes you are wearing; I have been looking at every young person wearing them clothes whilst driving since you left. You would not believe how many young lads match your description." Sue laughs as she says this to Mo. Mo was worried that she would ask about the safe or where he had been, but she does not mention it. She calls the office on her speaker phone and tells Sam to call out the doctor to the house.

When I get into the house I am helped upstairs into my bedroom. I get in bed with my clothes on, the staff team are not allowed to undress me or touch me as it puts them at risk of allegations of abuse. They cannot even give me paracetamol in case I have a reaction and my family try to sue the council if I die. I am given water and a bucket is by my side. I immediately throw the water back up into the bowl. I lie back on the bed and can feel Sue gently stroking my arm as I fall asleep or pass out. I am not sure which one but I remember coming round with the doctor saying I have food poisoning.

7

G4S

George

So I get back to Safe Stay at around eight o'clock. That prick Lee is not my fucking boss, he is here for my needs and that's it. I go where I want when I want. Fortunately for me, the tag guy from G4S was late. They have fitted the box but the security tag is faulty and they have said they will be back tomorrow to fit it around my ankle. I sign to say I have had it fitted for some reason and then go. Obviously this means I can go out and see my boys. Me, Ricky, Vinnie and Mo THE SPICE BOYS ha ha.

I speak with the manager, Jean and the worker, Daniel. Weirdly enough, I am back in the same room on the top floor as I was on my last stay. I wonder if the crazy girl who was here last time is still in the room next door. Laura, I think she was called, a strange one that one, I never could understand those goths?

"Okay George, welcome back. We need you to come down and sign your licence agreement," says Daniel. "We understand that you have not got your benefits in place and the staff member will apply for you tomorrow morning, is that okay?"

"Yeah, but I am on the sick."

"I know, so you will have to book an appointment at the doctors to get a sick note for a month. We will also have to apply for your housing benefit too. Do you have any ID with you at all?" asks Daniel.

"No, I have nothing," I mutter back.

Daniel tells me there is some mail still in my file from my last stay and the clothes I left behind are also in the storage. I am not arsed about the mail but I do want my clothes. I left some Nike 110s and some trackies.

Daniel walks into the office and I go into the kitchen. There is a lad and a girl there; she is cooking some food and the other is on his iPhone.

The expensive iPhone triggers a warning in George's head, as no one in Safe Stay has an iPhone unless they are non-drug user/straight head who really should not be here in THIS place or they must be a scammer / grafter who is earning big money. George lies on the side of caution when he sits down on the opposite side of the table.

"Alright," says George to the lad facing him.

The lad looks up from his iPhone he is wearing jeans, and an Armani polo shirt, not the usual style of a lad his age, which George figured to be around eighteen or nineteen. His hair is shaven and strawberry blonde, he looked healthy there is something he could not put his finger on about him. The shaven headed lad looks over his phone and replied, "Hiya!"

"Have you been here before? It's my second time being released from nick to this shit hole. How long you been here like?"

The lad looks over his phone again. "I am here with you people for eight weeks more, and then I hopefully will never see this place again." With that he got up from the kitchen table and left the room into the living room of the hostel.

He thinks he's fucking better than us! The girl who is frying eggs and bacon says to George, "I am Jessie, when was you here before?"

"I'm George, safe! I was here over a year ago I have been in the tents for a while and in nick. I have been bailed to here AGAIN! I'm gonna be on a 7a.m.-7p.m. curfew for the next few months like. What's the score with that lad, who is he?"

Jessie tells George his name is Bobby Martins and he is from a big family in North Manchester; he has just completed 3 years in a YOI for some serious charges. He was one of a gang of six lads who broke into people's homes, took their jewellery and then stole their cars. It was originally all about the cars, stealing them to order but as they got better at their crime and became more confident they progressed to aggravated burglary, basically knocking on the door of the houses and robbing them when they was actually in their homes watching the TV soaps. The story hit the national papers and the Manchester Evening News was all over it. The elder defendants were given 10 years plus, his 5 year sentence was only because of his age. He is also bailed here on a seven a.m to seven p.m. curfew like George until his risk assessment is lowered by the probation services and he can then be allowed to seek his own accommodation and his curfew restricted. They tied a forty-eight year old man up and beat him so bad it left him deaf in one ear.

When the judge passed sentence at the trial, he called the gang "a danger to modern society" who shown no remorse for their actions whatsoever.

George decides to stay in Safe Stay for the rest of the night; there are a couple of the residents who he recognises from the smoking shops and he ends up in one of the rooms having a smoke with them and telling them his stories about prison. He comes close to telling them he knows the whereabouts of a big stash of drugs. He heard his pad mate talking about it to his girlfriend on his phone, they were kind of arguing about her not going to collect it. There is a big chance it is still there as she dumped him on that call, grassed him to the police for having a phone in prison and said he was harassing her. They found the phone when they searched the cell as it was halfway inside George's rectum and he could not get it in time as they put the keys in the cell door and rushed in. George figures he will wait to meet with his boys and see what they say about the drug stash.

8

Social Workers

Mo

I am feeling a bit better today. I was in bed for two days, but I really need a joint I am sweating and twitchy. The staff thinks it is because of the food poisoning but I know it is because of the Spice. I have some spends that has been given to me. I go to the shop with the girl Sam and get some cigs. The owner is back off holiday now, so the kid with the spice is gone. The shop owner did not look too pleased when I asked where the other lad was who sells me spice.

I give her the rest of my spends and ask her to go to Elysium. She says her mate goes to the place in Old Trafford and she will go there but she wants a fiver for going and half my spice. I agree and she calls her aunt who picks her up and off she goes. I go back into the house and wait.

Jim and a woman called Claire are on shift. I don't know Claire but she seems okay. She tells me she was on holiday when I was here for the first week and she is pleased to meet me. Jim comes down the stairs and tells me that my social worker is coming to see me this afternoon. I am still not feeling 100% from the food poisoning and although my tummy is not a wreck through the spice I am starting to feel what I think to be a bad withdrawal coming on. I have not had this before, Ricky has spoken about it and so has Janey. It basically frightened me and the others so much we MADE SURE we got high on the camp every day as Ricky swears it was the worst five days of his life. Vinnie said the fucker was probably bullshitting just to keep us buying from him and he was just "scaremongering" whatever that means? I hope she gets back soon; I am dying for a joint!

I go upstairs and lie on my bed for a while. The front door goes and I hear Claire answer it. I run down hoping it is Sam and it is Janet my social worker.

"Hi, Mo. Are you okay?"

I like Janet she is okay, but it is really not the face I want to see right now.

"Yeah I am alright."

"I am just going to have a quick five minutes with Claire, are we alright to have a sit down in the living room together afterwards?"

"Yeah," I reply and go back up to my room. The front door goes again and I am down the stairs like Ronaldo. I answer and it IS SAM!

"Did you get it?" I say, but I can tell instantly by her pink blood shot eyes we are in business. BUZZIN!

"Yeah I have it," Sam slowly draws out. She passes Mo a previously opened gold bag of Spice 3.5 grams and half of a joint she has already rolled and smoked.

I walk out of the house and go into the back entry I light the joint and take a huge hit of it. I begin to feel myself slide down the concrete panelled fence which is actually the opposite side of the back yard of the care home. Sam has followed me around the back and says to me "How do you feel now?"

"Amazing," I reply and slouch onto the floor taking another hit. I pass out and wake to Sam shaking me.

"Mo. Mo. Are you okay?"

"Yeah I am alright, leave me here."

"You have banged your face; are you sure you are okay?"

"I am alright."

After a couple of minutes I come round fully feeling really calm and completely unaware of any of my surrounding and I have no care for it or anyone either. I love spice, I finish off the joint of the super strong gear with Sam and go back into the house.

"Where have you been, Mo we have been waiting for you for over half an hour?"

I walk past Janet in to the living room and ask Claire to get me a drink. The two of them are talking to me about where I have been living and staying and ask how they can help me settle in the house. I just mumble I am alright. Janet then gets to the point that that my mum wants to sees me and she wants to come to the house to see me. This gets my attention.

"What did she say?" I ask.

"Your mum is really worried about you Mo, a friend of your family has seen you begging in Manchester Piccadilly Gardens. They took a picture of you on their mobile phone and sent it to your sister."

I think to myself that I do not remember any of this. I have sat down in the gardens a few times of late and even went down to the village once but I cannot remember someone taking a picture of me, fuck this I am off out of here tonight.

9

Crack heads

Ricky

I am sick to death of crack heads and smack heads coming to the tents 24/7. The busiest times are about five a.m. when they are coming down from their dirty fucking drugs. Every fucking time they are asking for tick. Everyone is trying to take the piss out of me. Me and Janey have had about two hours sleep in the last week, it's beyond the joke. The time is flying by so quickly as we are always high. I am not sure why I am doing it as there is no money being made as we are smoking it as fast as we are selling it. I really cannot wait for this shit to be banned. My head is completely fucked and I can hear people saying my head's gone. I fucking hammered Joel's mate Dessie all over last week for saying I remind him of Preston. I made a mess of him too; apparently I have shattered his cheekbone and broke his nose. He was threatening me saying he will be back and all that shit, but this is my camp and nobody fucks with me here. A bonus about it all is my hands are okay now and I don't feel the sensitivity I had from when I broke them both.

"Are you awake?" I call to Janey, who is lying on her side with her back to me; she is sporting a black eye from the melee the other night. Apparently I hit her when I was leathering that prick.

"Yeah, what's up?"

"I need a shower. Are you going to come to the drop in with me, we can get a breakfast there too I am hungry."

"Yeah, I need to shower as well. I need some towels as well; I have finally had a period. Wake me up in a bit." With that, Janey goes back to sleep.

I go out the tent and shout to Vinnie. "Vinnie, you up pal?"

Vinnie is sleeping in a tent on his own. It was Joel's tent but he fucked off with that Dessie lad after the other night and has not been back since.

"Yes, pal I am awake. Come in."

"We are going to the drop in later for a shower and breakfast, are you coming?"

"Yeah, I am minging. I need to get some clothes from the basket in the laundry and do a clothes wash."

The YPSF has a large basket of donated clothes, this time last year Vinnie would not have dreamed of rooting through it, yet now he is actually planning to use it…

"Alright pal, it's Tommo have you got any gear?"

"Yeah, what do you want?"

The smack heads appear like fucking banshees. I did not hear him approaching or see him, yet he is three metres away from me.

"Yeah, what do you want?"

"Do us a tenner's pal; you couldn't lay us on another tenner tick as well, could you? I will sort you out tomorrow pal."

"NO. Stop fucking asking as well; I am not here to run a charity or be a social worker I am doing this for the money 'or to feed your own habit'," I hear Jarek say from a couple of tents down. The cheeky bastard. I will have him too before I fuck all these scruffs off.

"Alright, Ricky mate, no problem it was just that I could do with a bit more like and I only have a tenner. The smack head pays me in £1 coins, and smash totalling up to £9.83."

I look at his hand as he pays me, they are all dirty, chapped and rough, his nails are black with the dirt, it's disgusting. I look at mine as he pays me the money into my hand… They are exactly the same as his.

10

Solicitors and Cardiologist

Vinnie

I have been staying at my sisters for a couple of weeks just to get myself cleaned up and my head sorted. Lisa does not mind me being here for a while as she can see that I am alright (not that I wouldn't be) and the kids like to be around me because I am always up and on the go with 'em. I suppose sofa surfing is better than rough sleeping, but both have their positives and negatives when I think about it. One of the good things is I have got my benefits sorted out and can give her address to send my mail. As I am classed officially by Manchester Council as a rough sleeper, I am entitled to have an address for mail to be sent to without the benefits team threatening my sister with having her housing benefit cut as it looks like I am living there.

We have had a letter from the solicitors asking for us both to attend a meeting with them which I think can only be good news.

"Lisa, what time have we got to go up there?" I ask her.

Lisa is in the bath having some genuine "ME" time. She does not get a second to herself and thanks god for Vinnie turning up for once. The stress she has been under with the kids of late is unbearable. She split with her partner nine months ago and he has not been seen around the area, or on social media for that matter, since the day he went. She opens her eyes out of her relaxed trance in the steaming hot Radox-filled bath and shouts back to Vinnie who is at the bottom of the stairs, "One thirty, Vin. Do you want to take Ellie and Jess to the shops for some sweets while I get ready? There's money in my purse in the kitchen, will you get me some cigs, milk, bread and Rizlas as well?"

There's a pause and Vinnie replies, "Yeah."

Lisa can hear Vinnie getting her kid's coats on and thinks that he really is a good lad, a good dad in fact; before the break up with Maria he went to work on nights order picking at an industrial estate. He always sold weed and had lots of scams here and there, but his problems really started with the use of cocaine which lead to the breakdown of his relationship, not that I ever liked her much anyway. She was there for the good times alright but whenever he had a problem she dropped him quicker than a ton of bricks and went back to her mam's house until he had "dealt" with whatever shit he had put himself in.

After the breakup he got into a terrible fight and left someone in a bad way. Along with this, they raided the flat and he was also convicted of dealing coke and weed. It was all his own doing, high on cocaine and Vinnie accepts this. He was never the same upon his release. He became paranoid and on edge all the time; he had a drug debt to pay and the loss of raising his kids really affected him.

Lisa lays her head back and tries to get back into her tranquil state of mind. She lights the joint and takes a hit of the Spice that Vinnie gave her, it's really strong, she feels like she is going to pass out... A sense of panic comes over her and she jolts her body upright from the laid back position she was in. FUCK ME she says to herself, I love nothing more than a joint and silence when I am in the bath, but this is fucking awful, not the drug of choice to relax with for her.

I return back from the shop with the kids. Lisa is drying her hair upstairs and the kids are quiet, eating their toffees. I flick on the telly, I have been watching a box set called *Game of Thrones* when getting my head down at night. Lisa told me to watch it as she loves it; it's really good if I am honest. TV is the first thing you forget about when you are living in the homeless camps. I kind of understand how much of an idiot box it really is, just meant to keep us in our place. It scared me at first how much I have missed on what's been going on around the world and all that I have not known about it, but then I realise none of it matters as in my world. The world continued to spin day after day, no World War Three in my face, no politicians telling me I am better off under their rule and all other bollocks.

I am about to watch Ned Stark get decapitated as Lisa walks into the living room.

"Turn that off in front of the kids, Vin, and you can have this back!" She hands out the joint of SPICE to Vinnie and tells him not to smoke it in the house.

"Whatever is in that Vinnie cannot be good for you, it is nothing like weed at all... I would say it is what I would imagine heroin to be like."

Vinnie just smiles, takes the joint off her, pauses the DVD as King Joffrey Baratheon has Ned executed.

"Crazy series this, Lisa. Cannot believe they killed off Ned – he is the star of the show."

Lisa smiles to him as she is another three series ahead of him.

"VALAR MORGHULIS," she says.

"What?" Vinnie says, all confused.

"All men must die! It gets better, believe me."

The neighbour, Annie agrees to have the kids while Vinnie and Lisa go to the solicitors. The solicitors is next to Spinningfields, one of the most expensive parts of Manchester and less than a quarter of a mile away from where Vinnie had been living for the last seven or so months. They get off the bus at Shude Hill and walk through the Arndale coming out on Market Street walking past Slaters men's suit shop. Vinnie notices that three tents have camped there. The weather is nice in Manchester and even though the tents are in the shade, Vinnie thinks to himself that it must be sweltering inside there. Chances are he probably knows who is in there and would usually shout towards the tent alerting them of his presence, but he has business to attend to right now regarding the financial pay-out he is to receive for the death of his father and the potential poisoning of him too.

They arrive at the door of the offices which are old Victorian houses, or whatever era it was when they filmed *Mary Poppins*. He was watching it with the kids the other day and this is exactly the same type of building. A young girl offers them a drink while they wait, Lisa refuses but Vinnie decides he will have some water as he has just smoked his last joint of spice, which he has to agree with his sister, it is a fucking strong batch. He feels wasted and his heart is thumping.

After around ten minutes of waiting Mr Mellor comes back in from his meeting (which is probably a bullshit excuse from him being back from lunch late) and makes his apologies. They both go into his office which has a couple of signed rugby shirts on the wall 'Carling' and 'Edwards' are on the back of the jerseys, no doubt he has paid over the odds for them at some auction raising monies for some cause. It could even have been raised to support Vinnie and his homeless crew as it is all charities that Lee and the others work for.

"Thank you both for coming to see me today. I thought it would be appropriate to speak to you both in person, rather than communicate over the phone or send a letter to each of you."

"No worries, pal," I reply. "I am always in the centre anyway so it is easy for me to get here if you need me."

Mr Mellor smiles with his mouth firmly closed and nods his head.

"We have two claims against Manchester City Council and Northwest Housing Association. First is the appalling and unnecessary death of your father due to the council's neglect of service leading to the carbon monoxide poisoning and the second claim is the poisoning you had been suffering whilst sleeping on your father's sofa. I am confident that they will admit neglect and look to settle the case within the next two to three months with a financial settlement from them. However, with the case against yourself Vincent I think we may have a problem as new facts have come about in regards to you living at the address and they will contest this."

"What do you mean? WHAT'S THIS ALL ABOUT?" I can feel my blood pressure rise.

"At the time when you claim to have been living at your father's house, you actually had a non-molestation order against you put in by Northwest housing and social services which means you should not under any circumstances have been at the house, as was stated to you when the order served in December last year."

I can feel my chest getting tighter and my breathing is becoming heavy, I am trying to speak but nothing is coming out. The last thing I hear him saying to me is something about them challenging it and they will take it to court to fight my claim, the room starts to spin and I hold my chest, I hear Lisa calling my name and it goes BLACK.

I wake up and gather straight away I am in a hospital bed; I remember being in the office and vaguely having an oxygen mask over my face in the ambulance. I think to myself what the fuck has gone on?

"Nurse, nurse," I call out. I realise I am in no pain at all when I speak which is a good thing I think? A nurse comes over to me and asks if I am alright.

"How long have I been here?"

She tells me I came in around two p.m. this afternoon, she says I am okay and the doctor will be round in the next half hour.

"What time is it?"

"It's just after six p.m. Your sister has had to leave and said she has left some money for you to get a cab back to her home."

I look down at my chest and I can see that I have had something attached at some point to my chest, as the round sticky tape things are still attached to me. I can see the doctor coming in with what looks like his apprentice / sidekick. He speaks with the nurse and approaches me.

"How are you feeling, Mr Keane?"

"I'm alright, I suppose? What happened?" I ask. I must admit I am a little shook up.

"You had what looked like to be a cardiac episode induced by anxiety and according to your sister you are using a legal high called SPICE. The good news is we have ran an ECG on you. We believe there is no immediate signs of any damage to your heart but we would like you to come and visit us next week so we can run some more test on you and answer some questions we have about the legal high you have been using."

I interrupt him.

"Why was I out for so long?"

"We gave you a sedative which let you fall into a deep sleep. You were very manic when you came here – I start to remember me kicking off getting out of the ambulance – and understandably you were in shock. I am happy to discharge you and have made an appointment for you to meet my colleague next Monday so we can find if there is any genuine evidence between your drug use and episode you have just had. You are not the first person this has happened to who is using the legal highs and we really are concerned but cannot give

140

out facts to users until we have done a full study on the side effects."

"So can I go then?"

"Well yes, but we will want to see you on Monday."

"Okay," I say and with that I get my gear and go... I need a joint!

11

Lucky Me

George

The G4S have not come back to fit the tag on my ankle which means that I don't have a curfew. The good thing is the staff don't know and have probably forgotten about it too. I have waited in three days and I am now off from here back to the camps. I went to probation yesterday and so don't need to go until next week but obviously I am not arsed if they nick me anyway, I will do what I want. I jump on the Metrolink into town; I am going to the drop in first as I think they will all be there. I don't have any money at all I am fucking skint so I am going to have to rob something or someone soon.

The city opens up as I get one stop away from the centre. The weather is warm and the sky is blue. I like Manchester when the weather is nice like this; it's like going into a completely different place in the summer months as opposed to the winter months. In the winter everything is grey, the clouds are low and the city seems like it's hibernating in a miserable reality, just waiting for the clouds to part for the ten days of summer it usually gets. Not that this bothers the Mancs, as they crumble after around a week of sun and pray for a bit of "over cast" as they call it!

You get off in Piccadilly Gardens and you are confronted with a 12 ft high wall that wraps itself around what used to be a garden, even now in the summer months you have to wonder why they decided to put it there. Piccadilly Gardens are now a haven for me, my mates and the lads who sell drugs to us. They put a police box a few months ago to stop the dealing and begging, but it is only the odd Police Community Support Officer that is in there and they can only cover one situation at a time.

I can always get a ciggie off someone when I am here, especially in the summer. I just approach any person who is smoking and ask them, if the first or second person says no the third will say yes. The smoking ban has been great for cadging cigs as the workers all have to go outside the offices so it is easy picking. I walk up to a young lad who is chatting to the young office bird and ask him.

"You got a spare ciggie there, mate?"

At first he seems a bit taken back from me and he then gives me a look like he has seen me a thousand times. He opens his box takes one out and hands it to me without looking at me in the face.

"Cheers mate, have ya got a light?"

I light the cig hand him back the lighter and walk off, I hear him mumble something like, "I'm fucking sick of these scrounging homeless beggars," and then he goes on about the Council. I walk on without looking back; I have got what I needed.

I look out on to the gardens and can see a mixture of some beautiful women (where have they been all year?) and a few people who get drunk and stoned in the gardens all day. I let on to a few of the familiar faces and they nod back. As I get toward Oldham Street I see Simon and Rosie. They have lived on the step next to Morrisons for about five months. The step is in-between Morrisons and the cash machine and is a big enough earner to pay for their smack and Spice habits.

The issue Simon has is he is dead protective of Rosie because she is young and pretty and he thinks we all want to get with her; he really is fucked up that lad. He sleeps in the gardens because he has people after him for debts he owes and bad turns he has done to people. He actually thinks that because of the amount of CCTV in the gardens that no one will kill him there who he owes to. I see it different, if ten lads can sell any drug you want in the small area in the centre of Manchester without being approached then what's gonna stop someone doing you in?

"Are you going to the drop in?" I say to them both.

Simon looks at me and nods and gets up from under the pile of sleeping bags. They are surrounded with coffees, drinks and food, along with a cup with some change in it. They told me a while back that the Tuesday after Easter Monday is the worst day of the year for begging money. The cup was fucking empty all day and he ended up fighting and blacking both of Rosie's eyes. This caused uproar with the YPSF and supporting agencies who kept trying to lure her away from him with promises of a safe haven. Simon said he boxed clever, knowing that she is cuffed to the heroin and spice and is too scared to leave that more than anything. It seems cruel to me, but I am not in his position and I am not arsed anyway.

We walk up to the YPSF and share a joint of spice that Rosie has. Before Rosie and Simon enter they smoke some heroin in the alley. There is breakfast on but they won't be eating, they just want a shower.

"The other shower in here has been broke for the last two weeks. It better be open, I swear I will go mad. I could not get a shower last time as I had to go and pick up something and it was not open when I got back."

Rosie tries to keep the last bit of her dignity by showering twice a week at the YPSF; she can actually go any time she wants as Steve the manager of the YPSF is so concerned about her he has given her open access.

I get into the YPSF and sign in. I look on the register and I could not be happier Ricky, Mo, Vinnie and Janey have all signed in. Even Kane's name is on there.

As I am walking through the doors I can hear Vinnie go on about having a heart attack or something. I can see him sitting on the table with his feet on the chair; he is lifting his t-shirt over his head showing the lads his sticky patches that the electrodes were attached to.

"I swear down I was alright one minute the next my chest was all tight through the council bastards ripping me off with my claim. Just wait till I see them two new street workers the council have employed, I don't want no one talking to them about anything they can all fuc… YES GEORGE WHERE HAVE YOU BEEN PAL I HEARD YOU WAS OUT, COME HERE BRO."

I go over and hug him.

"Safe bro, how are you mate?"

"It's been crazy pal, all sorts has gone on, where you staying?"

"I'm back at Safe Stay, been there three nights, what about you?"

"I'm at my sisters. I got booted out of Elizabeth House for fighting with some crack head."

I order my breakfast and get a brew. Kane is chatting to Vinnie about the fight Ricky had with Joel's mate Dessie. Ricky can hear him and shouts over that he will get it again and that Joel will also be getting some for bringing the cheeky fucker to the camp.

Kane continues to me and Vinnie.

"Yeah man, this Dessie has been giving it the big one on the Oxford Road camp saying he is coming back to fuck him up proper with his own firm. The guy's a nob to me, but he was shouting his mouth off like snidey fucker intent on revenge."

Vinnie says nothing and I read it like he is saying 'not my problem' which is true, Ricky is a big guy, well he was anyway he can sort it himself. Mo is walking to the door and gives me the nod. I walk out with him without saying anything; I know he must have gear. The volunteer on reception tells us if we go out and smoke SPICE we are not allowed back into the breakfast area.

"I'm just going to buy ciggies, love." Mo lights up the joint.

"How are you, bro? Where have you been?"

Mo explains that he was ill and had to leave the camp. He went to his care home and got better then they said his mum was coming to see him and that there is pictures of him that has been sent to his mum so he got off this morning and come here.

"Good to see you, pal. Listen, I have got an idea about getting some money, wait till Ricky and Vinnie are with us and I will fill you in on it, but I know where there is a stash of all sorts of gear."

Vinnie, Ricky and Kane come out of the front door of the YPSF

"Aye aye sneaky fuckers coming out for a joint without sharing the love!" Vinnie is winding the two lads up as he lights his own joint of spice.

"Tell ya what, this gear is strong! It says on the bag 'insanity head fuck' it should be called fucking cardiac arrest after what happened to me last night!"

"My cousin says its panic attacks and anxiety; he went to the hospital too yo! Thought he was on his last legs, I told the boy he needs to chill some, you cannot be on the spice and the magic together it's a fucked up combi, yo!" Kane explains to his peers with a judge's right and authority.

The volunteer from the YPSF comes out and informs them all they are not allowed back into the drop in as they are smoking spice. The boys walk off up to Lifeshare for Kane to collect his ESA payment.

"Does anyone know where Heathbank Road is in Openshaw?" George asks the group. None of them know, but Vinnie and Ricky both know the Openshaw area very well and ask him why.

"I have a scam that can be pulled off but we have to be quick. When I was in there my pad mate was talking to his girlfriend about his 'stash'; he told her it was under the man hole of the back yard of the old lady's house next door. He was arguing with her because she would not get it and threatened her. She then rang up the jail grassed him up for having a phone and they turned our pad over. There was nothing we could do it was there and they did not fuck about. She wrote him a letter and on the back of the letter was her address. He thought he was clever, because he knew that even though I was in the room I would never know where his stash is. It could be all sorts: money, guns, ammo but his crack coke and heroin will definitely be there by the way he was screaming at her. I remember the address clearly."

For once the lads are all listening to him and he really is holding court. George is no leader by any means and he is really enjoying his five minutes of power.

"What's the address, George?" asks Kane.

"Like I'm gonna tell you."

"Listen, tell us the address and all of us will split it fair and sell the lot. I know people and I will get rid quick." Vinnie has his "carpe diem" head on him and really needs the money, they all do. They have nothing at the minute other than a tent. Ricky has a bit of debt to Jazz so is avoiding him until Janey gets her benefits, he realises he walked off and left her at the YPSF , but she will be ok as the girl Rose or Rosie is there and she can chill with her.

Vinnie is taking a charge hand role and says, "Let's go and Google the address now in Lifeshare and we will go and take it tonight, the FUCKING LOT MAN."

12

Blackpool

Lee is discussing the next panel meeting with the manager of the Lifeshare. He completes his business and then changes subject to his case load, currently known as THE SPICE BOYS! He originally said it to a colleague as a joke. It was overheard by Joel who is one of the young rough sleepers who penned the term to them when they walked in the YPSF one morning, since then it stuck with the staff and with the boys. As Lee is explaining how he has been challenged to get them engaging and back into supported accommodation they walk in... no member of society would really call it their lucky day when being approached by this mob, but to Lee it is like the chickens are home to roost and he cannot contain his happiness.

"Hello boys, how are you?" The lads rush straight past Lee, approaching Debbie, one of the staff workers and all ask to go on the computer.

The lads look like they are possessed and on something thinks Lee. He is half-right, they are high and if possessed it is only for the hope of an easy pay day. Debbie lets them on to the computer and Mo logs on. He is by far the savviest on the computer and is quickly on to Google Earth.

"What's the address, George?"

"32 Heathbank Road Openshaw M11 2JG."

George is right. The view show a row of large grey roofed terrace houses made from Accrington brick; houses that were built to last. Even the outside toilets that were built with them remain strong as the day they were built. Behind the houses is an alley that separates another row of houses with "brick shithouses" in the back yard too. They notice they will have to climb a steel gate that has been fitted to either end of the alley and then the dilemma of guessing which house it actually is – 34 or 30 as Sane's girlfriend lives at 32.

"Both of them won't have a fucking manhole so we just have to pick one of them, says Ricky, who now really does have his eye on the prize. He will rip these lot all off if he has to as he knows exactly where the address is."

Vinnie jumps in, "We will have to go late on tonight, get there about one a.m. when everyone is kipping. We all have to stay together today and go later. This is gonna be fucking brilliant if it pulls off." With that he cuddles George from behind and kisses his head at the back.

Lee approaches the group and asks about their wellbeing. Mo quickly shuts the screen down; Lee notices this with little interest.

"How are you all doing? Is everything okay?"

"Yeah," they all reply.

"Where are you staying, are you still at the end of Deansgate?" Lee asks casually.

"Yeah," they all repeat again.

"Ok I can see you don't need me for anything, but I just wanted to ask if you all want to come to Blackpool this weekend? It will all be paid for and we will get you all wrist band to the pleasure beach too"

No one answers Lee until Vinnie says he will go. –

"Yeah man I will come love Blackpool me."

They agree to meet at the YPSF at nine a.m. on Sunday morning; it is actually nine thirty the agreed time, but Lee always calls them thirty minutes early as they will be at least thirty minutes late guaranteed.

13

Stepping On Broken Toes

The posh soup kitchen is open every Thursday night in the Urbis square next to the print works. It serves up different food every week, from Thai green curry and rice to New York meat ball pasta served with bottled drinks that include strawberry lemonade soda and ginger beer honey soda.

The founders are Morgan Leahy and Sam Jones from Manchester's vastly prosperous Northern Quarter restaurant owners. This is their "I'm giving back" moment. The servers are the wives, husbands and social network of the owners, who are dressed down in designer tracksuits with blue surgical gloves over their hands. The kitchen is open to every homeless person in the city. It has become popular in its first three months and the Manchester Evening News has been all over it with pictures of Manchester's finest serving to Manchester's poorest. The response from the chief execs of the homeless charities in the city has been positive as they see this as a step forward with regards to support and awareness, as the restaurant owners all tweet about it continuously on the night and the next day. However, it is clear that the charities would have liked to have been involved with regards to advice and guidance and also used the engagement for their own records and network but they chose not to push the engagement further as "posh soup kitchen" made it clear that they are not stepping on their toes, they just want to do it their way for free and share the cost between the restaurant owners.

George is starving, he has not eaten since this morning at the drop in and all he wanted then was two slices of toast.

"What is it tonight?" he asks the lady who is organising the serving. She smells so good, her hair or perfume actually overpowers the delicious food that is just metres away from him. Her skin is clear and he cannot help noticing how thin her eyebrows are. She is beautiful in George's view.

"We have a choice of the vegetarian Malaysian curry with noodles or chicken pasta with Mediterranean vegetables with garlic bread. There is a selection of soft drinks," the lady informs him with a warm smile and nice tone to her voice.

"Oh right, cheers." He decides he will go for the pasta, he is not into vegetables so the curry did not appeal. George takes his drink and walks over to Ricky, Mo and Vinnie who are lying on the grass eating their food in plastic containers. Kane follows George as he was behind in the queue.

"She was gorgeous wasn't she? I wonder what she does for a living I bet she is loaded, did you smell her hair and perfume. WOW!"

"I know, man. I could see by the way she was staring at me she wanted a bit of the Kano loving."

"Fuck off you dickhead, she would not go near you mate," George says defensively.

"Where did you get all them drinks from Vinnie, they only give us one each," Kane ask with intrigue.

"I nicked 'em," Vinnie replies without looking up from his food. "After this we can go for a mooch around town and then we can walk up Ashton Old Road at about twelve o'clock." Vinnie is scamming, planning and over thinking his mind is in full throttle in apprehension of tonight's job.

Vinnie has noticed the police wandering about and a van has been parked up since their arrival. He knows the others have noticed too, but are keeping their paranoia to themselves. Two officers get out of the van and walk over to the soup kitchen, you can instantly feel the edginess of the homeless community, as everyone here, around thirty people has been involved with the police in the last 12 months and always have something of concern in the back of their mind when the police are about.

Everyone is watching them like a herd of buffalos when the lions are on the prowl. There is a low mumble amongst the groups. Vinnie can sense Kane is more on edge than usual. The two officers wander around the back of the lad's, then one of them notices Kane and comes towards. Kane shoots off like a rocket and heading towards the line of serving tables, he attempts to jump the table that the big metal food containers and drinks are on, he jumps too early and lands bad on top of it bringing everything down with him crashing to the floor hard and the hot container with the curry going over the "beautiful lady". The woman screams in shock rather than pain, she is a mess. The police are on Kane quicker than a lion on a buffalo.

"Kane Dawson. I am arresting you for failure to attend court on the 15 July 2000 and…"

With that Mo, Ricky and Vinnie shoot off towards Victoria train station and then around the back of the arena stopping when they get close to Bury New Road. For some reason they always end up close to Elysium.

The lads rest up near the shop and quickly head back down towards Deansgate. Ricky still owes Jazz money and he cannot be arsed with the hassle of him confronting him. With the job ahead of them tonight and Kane not here the lads all see the positive that there is one less person one less split. They laugh as they recite how he tried to jump over the table.

"What was he thinking; he was a mile away when he took off into the air the mad fucker." Ricky can barely get his words out.

The boys start to walk down to the house at around eleven thirty; it is a warm night and they have a nervous energy with a slight paranoia about them. Ricky seems on edge more than most and is smoking spice like the ban is coming in tonight! Vinnie has his organisation head on him.

"Listen, we need to be quiet on the street. We will go to the front of the house and get the number and count the houses to the end of the row. Me and Mo will get over the wall of house number 30 and you and Ricky look over 34 and be fucking quiet! Don't mention anyone's name when we are there either I don't want to be nicked because my name was mentioned."

All the boys are wearing black tracksuit bottoms, apart from Mo who has a grey tracksuit. The colour code was not planned; it is standard street wear for the kids of Manchester, it just so happens to go hand in hand with night robbery attire.

They arrive on Heathbank Road around twenty past midnight. The lights are off at 30, 32 and 34 they count eight houses along and figure will count the same back in brick shit houses when in the back alley.

Mo manages to slip under the bottom of the large metal gate which blocks entry to the alley, but Vinnie and George and Ricky have to climb. They walk slowly and silently up the alley. Vinnie jumps when a rat scuttles past him, but regains his stealth mode immediately. He lifts Mo up the wall which is about 6 foot high with a pointed grey-like brick on top which he always thought was put in these walls with the purpose to stop you climbing up it. The grey brick was always smooth and you could never get a grip when trying to get over it when he played hide and seek as a kid. He cursed the back alley walls as a kid and it wasn't until he was around ten when he finally mastered climbing them all with aid of the council's new big grey wheelie bins.

"Can you see it Mo?" he whispers.

"No," Mo whispers back. He looks towards Ricky who is lifting George over. George sits on the pointed wall and nods. Vinnie's stomach jumps in excitement. He lifts Ricky up and in turn Ricky and George lift both Him and Mo on to the wall. Ricky gently lowers himself onto the wheelie bin and drops down with superb ninja like athleticism. The others gently drop down bending their knees as they land to lessen the sound of impact.

Vinnie takes a plain-nosed screwdriver out of his pocket and tries to find a wedging point. It takes around a minute to find it in the dark. George can feel his bowels moving. None of the lads have strong bowels since they became addicted to spice and George is not 100% certain he will hold out with the nerves and adrenaline kicking in. George lifts the cover off; it is heavy as he moves it; he can see a bag.

"Buzzing," says Mo, who immediately jumps down into the manhole which is the direct pipe line for twenty homes' toilet waste. He lifts up an Oakley rucksack which is fairly heavy. *This is a winner* he thinks to himself. The lads pull him up. George's hands slip and he drops the cover. Ricky screams as the heavy metal cover lands on his toes. Vinnie winces as he knows they must be broken. Without hesitation, each lad jumps onto the bin and over the wall. George is last in line, as he puts his leg over the wall to drop down, he notices a girl staring at him from the window of 32. He pauses for what he thinks is about ten seconds, but in reality it was just long enough for her to get a look at his face. George catches up with the boys and races past Ricky who is now limping and wincing in pain.

"You have broken my fucking toes you dozy prick."

George ignores him and rapidly climbs the fence getting as close to Vinnie as he can as he has the bag. He who has the bag has the money.

14

Bingo

I run up the street stopping to walk when I get to Ashton Old Road. The last thing I want is some over enthusiastic copper pulling me over for looking suspicious.

"Let's go and sit in the McDonald's," Vinnie says to Mo and George, whilst waiting for a limping Ricky to catch up.

"You fucking prick; how the fuck did you drop the cover on my foot?" Ricky then punches George in the face.

"Calm down for fuck's sake," says Vinnie. "I've got the bag here and we don't even know what's in it."

"I'm sorry I had to hold my stomach mate, I meant for the cover to rest on my leg, I swear I was going to shit myself!" George tries to explain to Ricky.

Ricky's face screws up tight. "You have as well, you dirty bastard. I can fucking smell it, for fuck's sake George what is up with you, that's fucking minging."

I can feel my stomach go weak and I am about to throw up, but I hold it in like the professional I am. He is one fucked up kid that George I don't think I will ever suss him out. We walk up to the McDonalds and I tell them we will check the bag in there.

I buy two teas for me and Ricky. Mo and George go into the toilet.

"Do you want to make a run for it?" I say.

"I would but my foot is in too much pain." With this Ricky actually cracks a smile and the elation of a well-planned job is beginning to kick in.

We sit down in the corner, the McDonalds is empty other than people going through the drive thru. I'm aware I am on camera so I don't want to open the bag too wide and will get rid of this bag ASAP. George and Mo sit down and I unzip the Oakley bag. The first thing I see is the money: five wrapped bundles of £20s I know that's five grand then I see the biggest block of crack I have ever seen, MY stomach may not handle this! There is also a lot of skunk weed in two screw tight containers a mobile phone and a GUN with a few bullets!

"Fuck me lads we have hit the jackpot here. There's a hotel in Ashton let's go there and stay there in case there is any heat on with this or the coppers. I am not getting lifted with this."

Ricky's face has gone from one of pain to one of greed. I can see the evil in his eyes; he wants his hands on this bag but he is not getting it. We will also have to decide what to do with the gun and bullets. The phone will be getting the sim card snapped and launched. I think I might throw the phone as well to be honest and as for the gun! I want rid. I am not even touching the thing with my bare hands. First things first though, a taxi and strong paracetamols for Ricky. I can feel myself smirk every time he screws up his face in agony, I have to admit I like seeing him in pain.

15

Your Money's No Good Here

Ricky

Ricky tells the taxi driver to pull into the garage, Vinnie hands him some money, and he gets out of the taxi, walks over to the window speaks to the woman on her night shift.

"Two packets of Nurofen Max, eight cans of Red Bull, forty Embassy Number 1," he usually goes for rolling tobacco or a cheaper brand of cigs, but not tonight. He remembers seeing one of the older lads smoking Embassy when he started going into the pub on the estate when he was younger. The cigarette box looked cool and the lad dressed really smart; he was someone Ricky always wanted to look like, dress like and even act like. He even remembers going into flannels to buy the same Armani shirt at Christmas.

Ricky comes back to the taxi window.

"I need another £20."

"Fuck me, what you buying Rick?"

"These garages are a rip off; with their prices everything cost more." I pick up a sim card, tenner's credit and some chocolate. There is a bar in the village hotel so we can have some beers there.

We pull up at the door, Vinnie pays the driver and we walk to the reception. The night shift worker looks at us and says good morning. We ask for a room, he taps his computer and informs us we will have to book two double rooms. I am not happy but cannot be arsed arguing so I just nod and look at Vinnie for agreement.

"That will be £89 per room and check out will be eleven a.m. tomorrow."

Vinnie hands him the cash.

"Unfortunately we can only take a bank card payment."

"What the fuck do you mean? We have the money and paying you up front."

"I am sorry sir, it is hotel policy. There is a Travelodge who may be able to assist you across the way I just cannot take cash payment; it is company policy."

My blood is racing and I want to spit in his fucking face, Vinnie just walks off. I know he is thinking the same but if we get any shit now we are in trouble, well he is anyway. We go outside to George and Mo who are smoking cigs and rolling a joint of spice at the same time.

"Fuck these, we gotta go over to the Travelodge."

We head over to the Travelodge, they try and pull the same shit, but the Eastern European guy who is working there could not give a fuck really. He tells us his shift finishes at nine thirty tomorrow and will take the cash £100 for one double room, but we got to be out before nine fifteen, plus he wants another £100 as a deposit that he will hand back tomorrow.

"Yes mate, I am happy with that, cheers." Vinnie gives him the money and we are off up to the room to count our treasure pot.

We have:

One hand gun,

Nine bullets

£4,740.00 in cash

And, according to Vinnie's former drug dealing eye, 2 and a half ounce of crack cocaine and 2 kilos of cannabis skunk.

I have taken nearly every drug known to man but I swear I have never felt as high as when I shot at some prick a few years ago. It is the best feeling ever. Every fibre is my body is saying keep hold of the gun, but I know we have to dump it. If it comes back on us it will get back to the owner and all the lads who have had it in their possession, especially the lad who was padded up with George and that could be bad for all of us. Vinnie starts to hold court again.

"Right boys, we can sling the weed ourselves and the crack no problem, but the gun we need to get rid of it. I say we dump it in the canal on the way back into town tomorrow."

At this point I have to jump in, "Listen, why don't we sell all the crack to my mate Dermo? – Vinnie looks at me knowing we have to have a side earner – and fuck off to Blackpool with Lee and stay there for a week. We can make plenty of money up there selling this."

Mo's face lights up, you can see the kid in him. A fucking week in Blackpool in a hotel to a sixteen year old is a big thing; I suppose it is for all of us to be honest. I cannot remember the last time I left the city of Manchester.

"What about Janey and Kane?" asks George, not in concern but the under tone is that he wants them to have nothing to do with it.

"I will just not tell her anything, she does not know about Lee's trip and Kane will probably be remanded to Strangeways in the morning, his solicitor is shite."

"I don't know about you lot but I am going to smoke some skunk tonight and I think it is only right that we have a good smoke of rock too." As he says this George has immediately started to put pin holes in the empty can of Red Bull. It is time to get high... Very high!

16

Relapse

George

I haven't smoked rocks for a long time; I was bad on it before I first went inside. I started selling it at first but then like you do you smoke a bit here and a bit there and before you know it you're nearly 10 grand in debt with one of Warrington's craziest drug dealers after you. It's basically why I moved to Manchester. I would be dead if I went back to Warrington. I think crack is the only other drug I like as much of spice, but it is so moreish and expensive. I take my first hit from the can.

Mo holds the lighter for me and I suck hard on it. WOW, it hits me like a fucking rocket. And I am on the roof gabbing away instantly. Mo is on it and so are Ricky and Vinnie. Fuck me I am rushing, I have another hit.

"So I was thinking why don't we just keep the gun and do a couple of robberies with it. Obviously if we box clever we won't get caught, not big jobs small ones with good money."

"Fuck off, George; you're off your nut." Vinnie shoots him down but he's laughing with it, for once the boys are actually together feeling good all at the same time rather than the misery of living in the tents freezing in winter.

Mo interrupts the banter. "What about Jazz?"

"What do you mean, mate? Mo says we should rob Jazz, he has lots of money and he is always in work so we can rob his house when he is not there. Ricky is on to this as well."

"Yes, Mo I want that fucking Rolex he had on his wrist. I bet that fucker is in his big fat safe in his house. We can follow him home one night; that fucker deserves it. He is happy to take our money so I am happy to take his."

Vinnie says, "The gun has to go no matter what."

"If this is on us the come backs are fucking heavy but I will rob that cunt's house with you all, it's fucking on boys."

Ricky gets a hold of the gun and is waving it about and play-acting robbing Jazz's house with the gun in his hand.

"I will shove this in his fucking wife's face. I could not give a fuck. In fact, there are a couple of people I would like to pop one at. I love the power of a gun it's a fucking rush I shot at someone a few years ago over a patch for drug selling. I missed him like but I still got £500.00 for it and the other firm did not come back. I have a good mind to rob that Dermo prick as well, fuck giving him our gear we can sell it ourselves man."

Ricky is high as a kite, and completely on another level. I give him another hit.

"This is fucking brilliant, let's go to a brass gaff I have not had a shag in ages, and Mo can pop his cherry."

The laughter fills the room again along with the scent of weed, crack and sweat from our bodies.

My heart is pounding but I'm not arsed, it feels great like on Spice the time flies by I want to stay here.

Ricky is now bouncing around the room and wants to get out, "I think we should go into town boys."

"Yes pal, let's do it and then book another room for tonight, then we can go and see Dermo around twelve o'clock and get back on it," says Vinnie who is focused on the plan.

It's getting light outside, we leave the room around eight a.m. and walk down, well more like bounce down, Ashton Old Road and get on the canal path into town. I have the gun and the bullets on me. Obviously I really don't want to throw it in so I think I will stash it instead, you never know when it can come in handy. We have a couple more hits of the crack on the way down; we have done quite a bit in already.

"I don't want to sell it all to Dermo. We should keep some and just sell him the two big pieces that Vinnie says are ounces."

Vinnie puts his foot down. "No way, fuck that we can have a bit but I want to at least sell him an ounce and a quarter. I want a grand for it. £500 an ounce is the lowest I am taking, it is really good gear."

I throw the bullets into the canal, keeping hold of two, then stash the gun at the bottom of the wall behind a tree and cover it with grass and rocks. I note to myself that there is some graffiti art work on the wall where I store it, of a woman from the film *Misery*. I watched it years ago and will never forget her. She was a fucking psycho. I catch up with the boys and tell them it is gone.

They are not really arsed. Vinnie and Ricky are talking to each other at a hundred miles an hour, about dominating the city and being the main men. Mo just looks at me, he knows the score.

We come off the canal at Ancoats and can see the Brass House, 50 metres ahead of us. I'm not really arsed about it to be honest, but those two are adamant and I suppose it will be good for Mo too.

The Brass House was okay, but I don't feel it was worth it to be honest. I enjoyed my breakfast afterwards more and I honestly think it was better value for money, if anything though it has chilled us all out. Ricky has gone and booked a room in the centre whilst we wait for him in the cafe. They won't have us all going in one room and will want us to pay for two rooms if we check in together. After the room is booked we go into JD Sports to get some trackies and trainers and then go to Primark for some socks and underwear. I had to throw mine last night as they were covered in shit.

17

Dermo

I ring Dermo and agree to meet him in the Wetherspoons in Piccadilly. We have a few more hits of the crack in the hotel room and go. We all have money in our pockets, new clothes on and drugs are a plenty. Mo and George still want some spice so they walk to Elysium to get some for the week ahead in Blackpool. Weirdly I am not too bothered about the spice right now; the want and need is just not there. I will have a few more blast of the rock today as it is mighty fine.

Dermo turns up and immediately spots me and Vinnie at the back with our beers. He comes in with one of his pals; I don't know him but have seen him about. The lad is wearing a Red North Face t-shirt and grey tracky bottoms. His shades are on top of his head. I notice he has got a pair of the Adidas Yohji Yamamoto Trainers. They cost around £240.00 a pair for the standard ones; this lad has Salford written all over him.

If this Dermo prick even thinks that I am gonna let him and his pal rob us he has another thing coming.

"Hello Ricky lad, you're looking a bit cleaned up from the last time I saw you pal, what's been going on? Have you finally got off that spice shit? I've seen some fucked up people coming out of the nick lately through that shit."

He shakes mine and Vinnie's hand, he does not know Vinnie but I can see he is thinking the same thing I thought about his pal which settles me a bit. I ignore him about the spice; he introduces his pal as Tommy. Tommy shakes hands with us and he has also got the beers in which is good for me.

We chew the fat about football and birds for a bit. They are both laughing at us for going to the massage parlour this morning, it's not like Dermo has never been in his life and he tells us he used be a regular at one his pal's dad owns.

"So what have you got for us then Ricky?" Dermo switches to business.

"Two Ounce and half of rock, pal and it's lethal."

"I fucking know, your eyes look like a rat in a drug testing lab ha ha!! C'mon then what do you want for it pal?"

"Make me an offer," I quip back to him.

Dermo starts the barter at £700 for the lot, I come back as if I have heard him wrong and say so that's £1,750 all in. Each ounce at £700.00 and £350.00 for the half?

"Fuck off, Ricky, you know what I mean."

"I know and you know what I mean as well. You can turn this into 3 bag no problem when you sell it into £20s"

"I tell you what Ricky I cannot be arsed with this shit, if it is as good as you say it is and bang on in weight I will give you £1,200 for the lot. Let's weigh it and sort it"

I am a bit taken back on how fair and cool Dermo is. I genuinely thought he would be fucking around all day. "Come up to the hotel room with us pal and we will sort it," Ricky says to Dermo and Tommy, he is feeling the adrenalin of the deal but trying his hardest to remain cool and composed, something that seemed natural to him in this situation just a few years ago.

We weigh it out and Vinnie's eye was out, positively in fact. There must have been closer to 3 ounce in the beginning. We cut some off and give Dermo just over two and half ounce for £1,200 and have a quarter of an ounce for us.

"Cheers Dermo, pleasure doing business, pal. Do you fancy another pint in Wetherspoons?"

"No, I've gotta get off pal, laters!"

And with that he goes out of the hotel room door and leaves with his pal. I am buzzing and so is Vinnie; we go down into the pub again and meet up with the George and Mo.

"So they weighed the gear and it was less than 2 ounce, we must have smoked plenty last night and Vinnie's estimation was under," Ricky explains to George and Mo.

"The good news is we got £800 for it and still managed to keep a bit of gear."

I give Mo and George £200 each and they are happy, no questions asked."

Vinnie gets the beers in and we decide to stay on the beer all day in town we will book another night in the hotel and go to Blackpool from the hotel room on Sunday morning. Of course we will be nipping back up to the hotel room every hour or so for a cheeky hit of rock. This is turning out to be a good weekend, the sun is out too. What a time to be alive in Manchester.

18

Travel Sickness

Lee

Lee wakes up; his thoughts instantly are on the next fourteen hours. He is hoping for the best but expecting the worse. Fortunately, his colleague Paul will be driving the seventeen-seater bus and Lee will be the passenger as co-pilot. The truth be known he should be in the back with Mike and Julie as there will be trouble ahead. Lee knows he played a good hand when nominating himself to be Paul's support in the front of the bus. We are taking eleven of the most prolific petty criminals Manchester has to offer on a day trip to Blackpool.

He did a trip to Blackpool around nine years ago with three young people who were in care. The train ride down was absolute madness and the kids refused to come home with the staff and opted for a police ride home at midnight. They figured they would stay and have a good time, they knew the system would have to return them in a car once they were reported missing from home so they were not worried or concerned in the slightest. The police officers who returned them said they fell asleep in the car on the way back to Manchester and sobered up a bit so they was not too bad company! There were two aged thirteen and one fourteen year old but had been in care for numerous years and no family would foster them at that age, so they was well institutionalised already. Two of them are now deceased; they stole a car one New Year's Eve and wrapped the car around a lamppost in the Hale barns area of Cheshire. The other child, Emma actually went on to be a social worker in Birmingham.

I choose to take a bus into work; they are meeting us outside the Lifeshare building. I have all the documents needed for the day including the risk assessment. I copied it from an old trip to the Lakes I went on with the programme a few months ago so it did not take that long to re jig. Mike and Julie will bring drinks and sundries for the trip whilst all Paul has the responsibility of making sure the mini bus is clean and full of fuel. Best thing about this job is the team. We all support each other when needed. I am feeling a little guilty about sitting in the front now, but I suppose it's a job that needs doing and I got the option first.

As I walk down an alley off Ancoats Street I can hear Vinnie. Wow that kid is loud. I also hear the rest of the group too! That's concerning as it means they are all still up from the night before drunk and high or it could just mean they are excited. In fact it's just good to know they are here to be honest, they rarely leave the city centre and the funding we have is meant to be used to enhance their wellbeing and give them opportunities.

Lee can see the spice boys along with his three colleagues and five other young people he recognises from the supported accommodations around the city who are also on the programme and are supported by Mike, Julie and Paul.

"Hello everyone, good to see you all here," Lee addresses the whole group.

"Where have you been man? You're fucking late, ha ha!" Vinnie is in good spirits.

Lee looks down at his watch: he is late. "Jesus," he says to himself, "how long was that bus ride?"

"Nice trainers, boys. I see you have all smartened up for the trip and new tracksuits, who has won the lottery?" Lee gives a bit back to the boys, but quickly decides not to get too involved and not to ask too many questions.

Lee can smell the stale tobacco mixed with skunk weed and alcohol which seems to be sweating out of them. These lads never usually smell of cannabis? Lee glances at Mo. Like always, he looks like he is drained and malnourished, if he ever auditioned for the role of the Artful Dodger he would get the part on appearance alone; everything about him says poor, hungry and possible killer. He laughs the least out of the boys, like something is churning away at his mind constantly. He is always polite and well-mannered and respectful to all of the workers and volunteers, which shows traits of his good family upbringing but there is something there that no one can put their finger on. Meeting after meeting with all professionals cannot figure out why he wants to be on the streets in the tents rather than at home with family or even in the care homes where he is given a superb standard of middle class living, the choice of any school, even free university education should he want it.

"How are you Mo, are you looking forward to the going on the Pleasure Beach?"

"Hiya Lee, yeah I am I have never been to Blackpool. I want to go on The Big One, everyone says it's top."

"Yes, it is mate, I will go on it with you. We should have a good laugh today."

The young people and staff get onto the bus. As they are about to leave Kane shouts from the end of the street, "YO YO wait for me, bro!" Kane starts to run but depletes to a jog and back to a walk within twenty metres. When he gets on the minibus he is straight into the boys with hugs and embraces and starts to explain his episode on "being nicked" at the posh soup kitchen.

"The fuckers lifted me for a shitty non-payment of fine warrant. I got battered off the feds in the van as well, yo. The horrible bastard was laughing at me and slagging my step dad off asking where is he now. The fuckers know what happened with him, they was winding me up saying I would probably get a bullet or a thirty stretch like him. I told him he was probably right as I would put one in his kid's head if I ever saw him on the streets. He fucking laid right into me but I was not arsed Yo, it means I won, innit. They tried having me for an assault on him as well but my solicitor fucked 'em right off in court. Anyway, the judge bailed me and I am getting a fiver a fortnight taken out of my benefits to pay my fine off. What happened the other night is all sweet yo?"

Vinnie interrupts, "speak later innit, bro."

Kane is delighted about this as this must mean good news and by clocking the boy's new clothes and the strong smell of skunk he knows they are on a winner!

The trip is twenty minutes into the journey, all are in good spirits but constantly asking to pull over for a smoke break.

"We are going to stop at one of the service stations ahead for a toilet break you can have one then, is that okay?" Julie who is a big smoker herself informs the group which is actually a hint to Paul that she wants a cig too. If she does not have a cig in her mouth she has a big vapour cig in her mouth. It is even on a lanyard so she can puff on it constantly.

Lee notes that George has not spoken for the whole trip and is looking a funny colour; he is sat on the driver's side two rows back with a young girl named Nessa in front of him.

"Are you okay, George, you seem quiet, pal."

"Yeah I just don't like travelli-" With the words still coming out of his mouth George projectile vomits over Nessa. It keeps coming out as she moves and screams the stench is awful, Lee can actually see a slice of gherkin on her shoulder which looks like it is from a Big Mac. Her hair is covered in vomit and Lee almost throws up himself when he sees the chunks of sick in between her toes that are on show from her sandals. The bus is in uproar!

Paul pulls over. Nessa is battering George, he is trying to fight back but her life has had her in some real shitty situations and trained her to be an excellent fighter. This, accompanied with her personality disorder means she is a handful to say the least.

"FUCKING THROW UP OVER ME WILL YA!"
SMACK SMACK She lands two clean hard punches on him. George's nose is burst open straight away. Mike pulls George clear, the other young people jump out of the back of the mini bus on to the hard shoulder. Julie wants to pull Nessa back but due to the stench and the mess on her she cannot go near her. She stops hitting George who instantly runs out of the back of the bus and she breaks down in tears.

"I cannot believe the scruffy bastard would do that I will fucking kill him. Look at the state of me."

Lee is outside the bus, he gets all the young people on the other side of the barrier. Mike and Julie are comforting Nessa and pouring bottles of water over her. Julie has brought baby wipes, a spare t-shirt and lots of kitchen roll. Experience goes a long way when on day trips with young people, especially the most deprived, violent and homeless. Anything can happen and does; in fact, this is not the worst thing to happen on a bus when Julie has been on a trip. Shit happens from time to time, *best to be prepared* she thinks.

The bus is cleaned up and swept out; the stench is still in the air and probably won't go away. The next service station is only five minutes away. Everyone gets back in holding their noses and heaving from their stomachs. George is sat at the back, Lee can sense the other boys are laughing under their arms, he sure hopes Nessa does not notice as she will quickly come out of her sobbing state and go back into rage mode where she is capable of ANYTHING. Lee is praying that he does not throw up too; his stomach is weak, since the time his family all got food poisoning on their holiday. It has never really recovered, *c'mon Paul, drive faster* he thinks to himself. He sees the green service station sign ahead along with a Starbucks and McDonalds sign, both strategically positioned to hook as many humans as possible!

19

Tower Spotting

The bus empties the second it halts.

"Wait in the service station entrance in thirty minutes, we will clean this up and go, so make sure you are all here," commands Paul. Julie takes Nessa to the shower room. Mike gets coffee while Paul and Lee go to buy some cleaning products. The plan is to speak with the staff at the service station and borrow a mop and some cleaning products.

Kane is straight on to the lads for details about the job.

Vinnie tells him, "We got a few hundred quid for a bit of rock we sold to Dermo and we have a load of skunk here."

"I know man, I knew I could smell it how much have we got?"

"WE?" interrupts Vinnie.

"Come on, yo. I am in it too."

"A few ounces, we are gonna stay here for the week pal get a B&B and chill for the week and sell the gear," Ricky tells Kane.

"I want a blast of the Al Capone," says Kane.

"What's that?" says George.

"You know, stone, rock crack! Break a brother off some boys. A blind man can see you have been battering it all weekend."

The boys laugh together.

"I want one as well," Mo says.

"Okay, I will sort it." Ricky breaks off five pieces: three small ones and two bigger chunks. He hands out the three bits to Kane, Mo and George who scuttle off to the disabled toilet like the anthill mob.

"What we gonna do about Kane," says Vinnie, "is he in on this or what?"

Ricky contemplates, "I suppose so. He could sell sand to the Arabs when he is on form, if we keep him high he will have everyone in Blackpool buying weed off us in forty-eight hours. George and Mo have got the trade skills of a donkey so they can be spotters and holders for him. Our role will be to sit in the Wetherspoons on the front of the South Pier drinking cold beers, chatting to the ladies, taking the monies and controlling the operation."

"Deal."

With that Vinnie and Ricky shake hands and make their way to the toilets. They deserve a hit after all they have just endured on the minibus.

Kane makes his way back to the minibus, he feels like he is floating. "Fuck me I am flying? This is really good gear." Hs confidence is sky high and he starts to chat to a girl he has seen at the YPSF called Gemma.

"Yes gal, what ya saying? Are you coming on one of the rides with me, The Big One?" He winks and smiles expecting a positive response.

"Mate, you are wired, you better chill a bit as you will get thrown off the trip; they are not fucking daft, they can tell when someone is off it and will not have it!"

"Yeah, am I that bad whoa! I just had a toot of rock in the bogs and boy it is strong!"

"Good for you, not my thing like, that shit only ends in tears. Ask any crack head that's ever lived, mate. Listen, just chill for a bit ok. I will have a smoke and a laugh on the Pleasure Beach with you later, but for now can you give my ear a rest okay!" With that Gemma gets on the bus leaving Kane in his place and feeling a little paranoid.

The bus has been cleaned up; everyone is getting back on and relived to smell disinfectant. Nessa's hair is wet and tied back in a ponytail, you can see she has made some attempt to dry it on the hand driers but given up when the frizz started to kick in. She is wearing a sky blue t-shirt that has a picture of a hill and the words "The Lake District" written underneath it. She has a pair of beige three quarter length tracksuit bottoms on and a pair of cheap Velcro fastened sandals that the staff team have bought her. Vinnie is about to tell her she looks like one of those old people who model in the supplement of the Sunday papers magazine, advertising old people's clothes. There is usually an advertisement for a walk in bath on the opposite page to confirm to the reader who they are targeting but thinks twice when he looks at George and sees the bruising appear over his eye and bloody nose!

George has not even washed his mouth out from being sick. He bought a bottle of coke and drank that to get the sick taste from his mouth. His personal hygiene is awful; he even had an abscess in his mouth a while back and would not go to the dentist or doctors it swelled up like the Elephant Man. Janey gave him some of her unused antibiotics and it eventually went down.

"I just don't understand that lad, he does not care about himself one bit, yet at the same time he would kill for anyone of us? How is your eye, George?"

"It is okay, Vin, I just took a pain killer in the toilet."

The lads all laugh at the joke together leaving the others including Julie and Mike confused at the joke. Vinnie whispers to George, "She has calmed down a bit, give her some spice as an apology for spewing your ring on her pal. It was bang out of order, I know it was an accident but I would have stabbed someone if they would have done it to me never mind a couple of cracks."

"I think she would have shot me if she would have had the means at the time ha ha!"

George takes an opened bag of spice out of his pocket; there are a couple of grams in the bag. He walks up the minibus and sits next to Nessa.

"Sorry about that before, it just came up, I couldn't hold it down."

Nessa is about to snap back viciously but sees a bright gold shinning bag being passed to her discretely from George. It is SPICE gold, she knows straight away and at the same time her rage changes to thankfulness. She is not the biggest spice head in the supported accommodation she lives in, but she has a smoke every day now; it's normal, everyone does.

"It's alright, forget about it. To be honest I just want out of these geek clothes. There is a Primark in Blackpool and Julie has promised to take me there when we get off the bus. I look stupid in these."

"No, you look alright," George lies.

The banter begins to swing again and the excitement is getting to the young people who in their lifetime have probably never left the little England they live in, unless they was in foster care and was probably taken away every year. Lee has done this route a million times or more as the in-laws own a caravan on one of the sites in Blackpool; he knows the Tower will be in view in the next five minutes.

"Okay guys the first person to spot the tower gets £10 cash."

This brings the attention of the bus, Mo looks out of the left hand side of the bus searching for the Tower with eagerness.

"It's on this side, you daft twat," calls out Vinnie.
Everyone's head is looking for the Tower then George spots it!

"–It's there."

"Where?" Responds everyone.

"Behind the trees, it will come into view in a minute."

The trees clear and George points to a tower in the not too far distance. The bus goes into fits of laughter, even the staff team join in. George has identified an electricity pylon as the tower; his embarrassment is showing on his beetroot red face.

"That's a pylon, you thick fuck," Arrrggh ha ha ha Kane is on the floor.

Then Nessa spots it, "THERE IT IS THERE." Her misery has gone and she is declared the winner the Tower is in sight and they have made their journey.

Part 3
A Hub for the Homeless

1

Aggressive Begging

Janey

Aggressive begging! WHAT THE FUCK DOES THAT MEAN! All I asked to the lad was if he could give me £1 to get home as I needed the bus fare.

I had been having a drink and a few joints of spice in Piccadilly Gardens with Rosie. We were laughing as we walked through heading towards Princess Street. I saw these two young student lads sat down with their matching skin tight jeans, striped t-shirts and shades on (why they was wearing jeans I don't know it was boiling). I said 'hiya' all nice and everything; they responded 'Hi' back but did not look up.

I said, "'ave ya got a pound to help me get the bus home?" He said 'no' and I carried on walking. He then called me a scruffy cow under his breath so I turned back on him. He thinks because me and Rosie are girls we are not going to stand up to him! I turned back I told him straight not to take the piss out of me cause it ain't gonna happen! He shits himself and starts apologising with his hands up covering his face. So when he cowered I fucking hit him in the face to let him know who I am. I was shouting louder then, putting him straight and in his place. A do-gooder comes over and tries to calm me down and gives me the pound I needed. I thanked her and gave him a quick stamp on his belly before I left to teach him a lesson. Some bastard videoed it on their phone and it is now all over Facebook and in the paper. The police came to the tent today and arrested me for assault and "aggressive begging". I am now sitting in this cell and will be here until Tuesday morning to appear in court.

Ricky has disappeared all weekend, someone has said that they have probably gone to Blackpool, but the trip was not until this morning, so where have they been until then? I am sick to death of this life, why me! I scratch into the wall paint "Janey" and then try to get some sleep. I can feel the cold sweats coming over me.

2

The Pleasure Beach

Mo

Julie gets us all to wait in the reception of the pleasure beach whilst she gets us our wrist bands. I am excited by it all. I was really tired on the last bit of the drive because we have not been to sleep since Friday. I probably got about thirty minutes in the hotel at about five o'clock this morning but with all the crack we have it keeps you awake. The spice made me feel better when it was wearing off and I was getting tired it eased the come down of it. I like spice I have always said spice is really good the only downside is the dodgy tummy, aches and pains and I think I am not as clever as I was, I sometimes cannot think proper or understand things like I used to. It is hard to explain but I think it is my head not being right, that's what everyone else says about themselves in the camp.

"Thank you, Julie," I say as I get my band.

"You're welcome, Mo. Have yourself a good day and we will see you at one p.m. at the food court area for lunch."

Lee walks over to us and asks what "we" are going on. We tell him "laters" and leave him there.

I felt dead tight because he organised it for us, but George said fuck him as he asks too many questions and we don't want to be seen with a carer, we will look like a bunch of not rights!

We head over to The Avalanche ride, the queue is big so me and George wait in the queue while Vinnie and Ricky go to the toilet and get a drink and Kane disappears with the girl he was talking to on the minibus!

"They are taking the piss out of us, Mo!"

"What do you mean?"

"They are having a hit of the gear while me and you wait in the queue for twenty minutes and then they will come back and just get on the ride."

"I did not realise, I thought they was being cool because they was getting us a drink."

"Don't worry about it, George we can smoke the spice in the queue and they are bringing us a coke back."

The boys come back within ten minutes with two cokes, they have drunk half, but Vinnie says they are big drinks and nearly four quid each so it is better to share. We finish another joint and go on the ride. It was brilliant. The best feeling ever, well nearly but I loved it and wanted to go on again and again, but Ricky said we had to go over to The Big One while it was not too busy. Me and George queued up again while them two got more drinks.

I went on The Big One, The Avalanche and The Grand National, had some rock (not the Blackpool type as Vinnie keeps saying) and smoked a big joint of spice… and then I saw the laughing clown! I did not think it was funny, it actually scared me; I mean what was it laughing at? They have all seen it before, but I hadn't, so I just stared at it for ages and ages until they started shouting me from near the water ride. I moved on away from the clown, it was still laughing, at what I don't know some things just don't make sense to me.

We all met up with the rest of the trip. Lee asked us if we were having a good time. I was, I really was, apart from the clown.

"Okay guys, where do you want to eat?" Lee asks the group.

"Let's go to the Burger King, Lee." Vinnie nominates for us.

I am happy to eat anywhere, I'm not hungry really, I want to carry on with the rides but it is best to stay together I suppose.

Ricky has left the Oakley bag on the bus with the skunk weed in it. He is telling us that when this is finished we will pick it up from the van and get off. We will book for a B&B for the week and decide whether to go back up to Manchester or stay on for a bit. We all eat our food and drinks and leave Lee who asks us to meet him at Valhalla at four p.m. No one says thank you and they all just leave their trays on the table. I say thank you to Lee and help him put the trays away.

"Why did you not have any food, Lee? Do you prefer McDonalds to Burger King?" Lee shudders prior to response thinking of the gherkin on Nessa's shoulder.

"I'm not hungry mate, I will get a coffee later."

3

South Shore View B&B

Vinnie

We have had a good day but we really need to take care of business straight away from here. I have been up for three days and a bed is what I need right now. I can feel my body is completely shattered, it is only the drugs that are keeping us going. I will be glad when all of the rock has gone; by the way Ricky and George have been hitting it there can only be a bit left, surely.

Kane reappears with his arm around the girl he was chatting to on the minibus. Fair play to the lad, his persistence has paid off with her. She is not my cup of tea but horses for courses as they say. I say this as the horses from the steeple chase ride fly past the two of them; it must be a sign I chuckle to myself.

"Yes Kaneyay, I see you have fell in love there pal."

Kane sees Vinnie who has caught him out, holding hands with the girl, he quickly removes his hand swiftly moves over to Vinnie with a strut of a champion and plays it off to him like he is just playing the "game".

"Nah man, I am just keeping her sweet, you know what I mean. Have you got any of that THING on you?"

"No, Ricky has it."

With that Kane is off over to the shooting alley where George Ricky and Mo are desperately trying to win an iPad.

I see Lee and the rest of them all coming to meet up.

"Are you ready or what, pal? Been waiting for you for ages we want to go."

"Hang fire, Vincent it's only just gone 4.25 and for a change, you are early."

Vinnie does not like to be called Vincent, but he lets this one go with Lee as his response was quick and funny.

We head off to the minibus and I tell the boys the plan.

"We will look for a B&B on the back streets – not on the front as they cost a fortune – and with it being the bank holiday weekend they will want to rip us off and I am not having that."

"Does that mean we won't see the sea?" Mo asks with the dream in his head since early childhood of waking up and seeing the Sea first thing in the morning.

"Yeah, we won't see the minging Blackpool Sea."

As we head into the car park Ricky walks ahead to get in the bus first. The door unlocks and he is in and out with the 2 kilo of skunk cannabis. It is in two screwed sealed containers which should keep the skunk fresh and seal in the smell, it does a bit, but you can still smell it in the bag. In fact, when they opened it the other night the smell was that strong it was like someone was actually smoking in the tub itself! The potency is good news as they won't have trouble shifting it and return customers will be guaranteed due to the high Tetrahydrocannabinol

THC content added when it was grown, probably in a terraced house in Manchester with the electricity being wired direct from the mains by the farmer (George's pad mate) costing him nothing. I think to myself as in life and especially in this case someone's loss is always someone else's gain!

"We are getting off Lee, we have decided to stay up here," I tell him.

"What do you mean you're staying up here?"

"I mean we are staying in Blackpool and not coming back tonight or tomorrow, we are homeless we don't have to go or do anything... We have decided to stay here and that is that. Cheers for the lift but our trip is not over yet, come on boys let's go."

Lee looks to the staff team for support, Paul looks back at him and shrugs in a manner that says "there's nothing we can do to stop them leaving".

"He is right we are homeless and HAVE THE FREDOM TO DO AND GO WHEREVER, WE WANT. YOU THE WORKERS ARE THE ONES WHO ARE TRAPPED IN THE SYSTEM."

Lee starts to phone his line manager in panic, but he knows we are young adults, well most of us are and the facts are we can go and we do without even looking back. We have plans to make some money out of this shithole.

Blackpool Front is busy, after walking down it for an hour or so I notice that there are lots of people who are homeless or not able to support themselves on their own, the supported accommodation and "support worker" type of people. All I can see is future versions of George

Ricky, Mo and Kane and present versions too. I suppose beggars and drunks stand out to the regular tourist to Blackpool as all the same, but to us I can put them into categories on sight. I see young homeless runaways, drunks, drug addicts and drunks who are also drug addicts. The average age of a homeless person here is higher than in Manchester but saying that, anyone who has been homeless and addicted to drugs for over ten years will have at least ten years age added onto their faces.

It is like this is where all the homeless and failed people in society congregate. Once they have washed up and been disqualified from every support service in their town or city, leaving behind them a trail of housing benefit arrears from supported accommodation and a list of people they have stole and cheated from including the local drug dealer who swears to rip out their heart "if they ever catch them".

I suppose Blackpool has become a hub for all society's fuck ups and failures from all over Britain and listening to them right now we have a mini Scotland here. This is all good for us as we are amongst our own and there is always money to be made amongst your own people.

We notice a "smokers shop" with bongs and other gear in the window. Without even saying anything we all instantly walk inside like a magnet to a paper clip. There is a young lad behind the counter; he looks up at us taking his eyes off his phone screen. "Alright lads what do you want?" He immediately can see us for spice heads the way I identified the street homeless of Blackpool. I am not happy about this, but looking at the company I am currently keeping I suppose I can see his point.

"Do you sell spice?" George asks. His foot has barely crossed the threshold and he has his hand in his pocket for money (a fool and his money are soon parted).

"Yeah we do and magic, what do you need?"

"Just the spice please," says Mo.

The shop keeper pulls out some bags of "SPICE ARCTIC" and tells us this is a new version which is stronger than what's going; about an eighth is £25. George is about to give him his money before I interrupt.

"Look pal, the name on the bag means fuck all – you put that on the bag yourself. The spice comes already batched and the spice chemical is sprayed onto the marshmallow plant. We know our stuff and the current prices too. Can you do us two bags for £35? We are here for a week and looking for a B&B that is not too pricey, we will be your best customer."

I see him clock George's wad of cash and the lad looks a bit set back from my tone. I suppose I can be a bit full on when getting my point across but I have no intentions of kicking his head in, well at the minute I don't but if the fucker gets lippy he can get full force of my size nine in his head.

"Yeah okay lads, we can do two for £35 where are you lot from?"

"Bolton," I say quickly, before George and Kane give our life stories away, these fuckers will befriend anyone with Spice. It is not his business where we are from or what we are doing, his job is to sell and we are to consume. The chit chat can wait for another day. I buy two hundred snap bags for bagging up £20 bags of skunk. He tells us of a cheap B&B called the South Shore View which is a few streets behind the shop which should be able to get five of us in a room. He gives us the directions and sends us on our way. Before leaving he tells us he is called Joe and the shop is open from ten a.m. till ten p.m. every day.

4

Sleep Like A Baby

Ricky

We get to the address which is way back from the beach and practically in a residential area. I am knackered. I have had no sleep for what feels like a week but is actually four days. I am wired on crack and high on the spice, the two mix well together, if I am honest. I have to box clever with it as Kane, Mo and George are getting greedy and I want it to last a few days yet. Vinnie likes a bit, but is not as bad for it as me or the others. I can control the habit, I am not like these fuckers I am better than them; I have always said it and always will be. I am like a leader to them and they need my guidance which they will get at a price.

We will make good dough from the weed but we have to be on the ball. Managers and foot soldiers is the way to run this operation and I will execute the perfect plan with Vinnie and the low lives and drug seeking tourist will be ours to prosper from. But first I need a bed and a good rest.

Vinnie is first in to the reception, the smell hits him first, it is not dog or chip pan he can smell but something in-between the both.

"Fucking hell, that's minging." Vinnie does not even hide his displeasure for one second but what is surprising the bloke on reception is not even bothered. His frame is big and obese. He is wearing a cream shirt tucked into a pair of grey slacks. His belly is bulging over it and you can make out at the back of his waist he is wearing a belt. His sleeves are folded up to the elbow. His face is round with a couple of chins joining to his neck with a bald head on top with hair growing around the side. He looks like a modern day Mr Pickwick from the book Oliver Twist. Mr Pickwick stands up from the stool, which actually looks like it was being eaten by his arse as it completely covered the round leather support.

"How can I help you?" he says. Politely, but in an "I could not give a fuck" tone. I sense something is not right here but keep tight-lipped, I have seen these places before.

"We want a room for the five of us and we will be here until next Sunday at least."

He pauses before answering, "I can do a room with one double bed, two singles and will be able to put a camp bed in there too, how does that suit ya?"

"How much is it?"

"The room is £100 a night, for seven nights it is £700.00."

"Fuck off, you are trying to rip us off you cheeky fucker; it's £89 a room a night on the front." Vinnie does not hold back with his response or tone.

"That's fine then, go and book somewhere on bank holiday weekend."

"We will, come on boys I would rather stay on the fucking street than give you that money for this shithole."

The lads are about to leave and I say to Pickwick, "Do you want to offer us a deal, a student discount?" Pickwick looks at us, it's clear he can see we are no students, but the bluff has been placed by both sides and it is time to negotiate.

"Sorry boys I did not know you was students, you should have said. There is a special 30% student discount for you."

Both me and Vinnie figure that it is £490.00 total, whilst Mo, George and Kane stare blankly at Pickwick.

Four of us have to stump up £122.50 each as Kane has no money at all. Mo and George have no change, so they give me £125.00 and I tell them I owe them £2.50. I give Pickwick the cash. He hands the keys to us tells us breakfast is 7.30 - 10.30 every day and we will be charged £50 if we lose the key, the bastard takes a £100 deposit off us too!

We go up the stairs to the third floor, our number is nine. Pickwick even makes us carry the camp bed and bedding up too, what a fucker. The smell is awful and the carpet is sticky, this is where I suspect the smell is coming from.

"I think we are staying in one of the B&BS you see in Manchester that is not exactly for tourists, it is where the council send the emergency homeless, the kids who have left care, released prisoners and refugees!" No sooner do I say that when a drunken old man stumbles out of one of the rooms. He stinks of piss and whisky and mumbles as he goes past us on the stairs.

"There is no way he has paid £100 to stay here a night, we have paid to stay in a homeless refuge. If we reported ourselves homeless to Blackpool Council tomorrow there is a good chance we would have ended up here for free!"

Mo puts the telly on and we settle on the bed. Me and Vinnie take a single bed, Mo and George share the double and Kane is in the camp bed. There is no shower in the room; it is at the end of the hall next to the communal toilet. We smoke a couple of joints out of the window which is facing the gable end of a terrace house not five metres away. South Shore View my fucking arse. I lie on the bed and crash almost instantly into a deep sleep.

5

Pleasure Before Business

George

I wake up first. I cannot believe the time; it's half one, I never sleep this long. I just don't need a lot of sleep. Obviously it's because I am naturally fit, I always have been. Not needing a lot of sleep is good when you're on the outside, but when you are banged up for twenty-three hours a day in the nick it's a fucker I tell ya. I get myself up and go to the toilet. I make my way down the corridor and enter the small room. It has torn lino on the floor which someone has pissed on. Fortunately, there is toilet paper.

I return to the room and see that Mo is awake.

"Morning, George."

"Alright pal," I reply.

Vinnie and Ricky are like two zombies and are away with the fairies. Kane comes around.

"Fuck me, is that the time, must have slept for over twelve hours bro, are you making a joint?"

I look towards Mo who immediately starts skinning up. He takes a silver bag of SPICE ARTIC from his pocket.

The man in the shop was right, it is strong this stuff and it tastes nice as well. Kane goes to the toilet he is wearing nothing but his boxer shorts from Next and a pair of odd socks. He is long and thin, his skin colour is a pale white, yet his neck and lower arms have caught a lot of sun in the last few weeks. We smoke the joint and chat for a bit about what we are gonna do today, but we will have to wait for them two to wake up before we know properly. Mo is adamant he is going up the tower and I can see he is itching to get out there on the front.

Kane is high from the joint and is asking for where the rock is.

"It's in Ricky's pocket," I tell him. Ricky is asleep with his clothes on, we all slept in our clothes apart from Kane. Ricky is nudging, calling out in a whisper "Ricky" but he will not wake, so he tries to get his hand in his pocket to get the gear.

"What the fuck's going on!" Ricky wakes up.

"Yes bro, we have been trying to wake you for ages, we want some of the stone mate."

"What?" Ricky is confused and has not come round proper. "What time is it?"

"Ten past two mate, you have been away for a while, pal. You crashed around ten last night and have not moved, even Vinnie is still away."

Ricky passes them a piece of the crack cocaine and tells them to chill on it as it will leave them with two nasty habits.

"You should talk," George says back, "you have had your fair share over the last three days or so."

This is true, Ricky says to himself they both go well together and he considers himself to have good taste and the current taste is for crack cocaine and the legal high spice.

Vinnie wakes up; he stretches with a loud yawn.

"What time is it?"

"It's quarter past two," I tell him, "you have been a kip for hours pal."

"FUCKING HELL this hotel may be a shit hole, but the beds sure are comfy. We have made up for the last four days of now sleep at least." Vinnie's eyes scan for the Oakley bag with the skunk weed in it. He then gets up and walks out of the room to the toilet.

Vinnie returns. "That toilet is worse than the alley toilet on Brazennose Street." His face tightens up into a scowl as he remembers standing in the shit during the cold winter months, he never found out who did it, but the suspicions were on Janey.

Vinnie's head is buzzing, making calculations on the amount of weed they have and the return they can make while up here.

"Should we start bagging the weed up and then sort out who is doing what?"

Ricky cuts him off.

"Vin, it's a nice day, Bank Holiday Monday, we have money in our pockets and there is loads of birds out there, should we just go on the piss today and get a feel for Blackpool via a pub crawl. I know business should become before pleasure but let's gets to Wetherspoons and get on the beer all day and get pissed and wrecked and stoned!"

Vinnie contemplates this and says, "Fuck it, let's do it boys, but I want a breakfast first, I am starving and we

HAVE to buy three cheap phones for you, Kane and George so we can be in touch, this is a must today."

"What about me, don't I need a phone?" says Mo.

"Yeah of course mate, it's just that you are always with George no matter what. We will get you one too pal, with a camera on it so you can have holiday photos." Everyone burst out laughing as they put their trainers on and leave the room exiting on out of South Shore View B&B.

6

The Full Monty

Vinnie

I am really looking forward to the next month ahead, we have money in our pockets, drugs and spice in our possession and the freedom of Blackpool. I honestly feel like this is my time to get my groove back. I hope to return to Manchester soon but if things go well I am happy to stay here, get a flat with the council maybe get a bird and open a new Facebook account with another name. I have had a few accounts, I close them down when I need to disappear and open them up when things are good. I tried contacting her to see my kids via Facebook, but she kept blocking me, so I opened another and another and another. I had to come off it once I started living in the tents and hostels as I don't want people my area seeing me all fucked up on spice and homeless.

I am going to have to call my sister today or tomorrow to let her know where I am and what's happening with the claim off the council fuckers, I can feel my heart start to race as I think about it. I am still so angry and to be honest, I miss my dad, I miss taking care of him and I miss him telling me stories about my mum, he told the best stories 'bout her when he was drunk, he genuinely loved her and sometimes I wonder if the loss of her was part of his demise and maybe part of mine too. I don't miss my mum; I want for her but don't miss her. The memories are so faint I wish we had Facebook when she was here for videos and posts and stuff. Me and my sister have nothing but her pictures and a couple of coats she had, Lisa keeps them in her wardrobe, sometimes I go in her room and smell them, the scent is still of her and is the strongest sense I have of her.

"Vin, Vinnie are you there pal; you have not said a word for five minutes?" Ricky notices that Vinnie is very quiet as they are walking on the street to find a greasy spoon café.

"Yes pal, that fucking spice is strong mate, it has wiped me. I might need to have cheeky shot of rock after my brekky."

"You look it pal; your eyes are glazed over like you are filling up ha ha ha!"

There is a café ahead of them a street or so behind the South Pier it has a Union Jack sign and states that they do full English all day. The café is called Georges.

"This will do for us let's get a scran down us boys, it's on me."

The boys all thank me as they enter the café. I am determined to stay in good spirits, I have been doing the numbers in my head for the weed and a little side thing I will do with Ricky of course.

We all order the Full Monty with a pot of tea except Mo and George who order strawberry milk shakes. The food is really nice and we even order more toast. It dawns on me that in the last four days we have eaten a Burger King meal, I did not even eat to be honest; the crack and spice took away my appetite. As we finish up I ask the boys where we want to go first.

"I want to go up the Tower today, Vinnie, George is gonna come with me will you all come too?"

"How much is it, Mo?" asks Kane who is skint.

"I don't know, will it be more than a tenner Vinnie?"

"It's about £30 odd quid, Mo."

There is a silence amongst them as the cost is a lot that is two bags of spice.

"Go for it pal, have a good day. I will get some phones and me, Ricky and Kane will sort out the business in the pub and meet you later." Mo looks across the table to George for a response.

"Yeah I will go mate I am not arsed, obviously I don't want to pay, so we can see if we can scam it first then if not we will try and blag kid prices."

Kane is outside smoking a heavy loaded joint of spice; his eyes are so pink he looks like he has conjunctivitis. Mo and George go out to join him and I tell them I will pay the bill. Ricky waits with me.

"Ricky, listen pal, I have been doing the maths on the weed all morning in my head and I have a plan for a little earner off the side of our split pot with the boys, I will fill you in later about it but let's just say we will have a few quid in our pockets should all go to plan."

Ricky agrees and responds, "Yeah mate, we will talk shop when Kane is not about, but we must keep him sweet, let's throw him a few quid in advance as I can see he is not too happy that we are all flush and he is on his arse and even stinking a bit, his clothes are minging."

"Good idea my good pal, I am beginning to think you're related to me as your ideas are the same as mine, but the fact you're an ugly fucker shows there is no genetic link."

As I laugh at Ricky he throws a dig to my arm, we go out the café leaving the money for the bill on the table and even leave a 60p tip, and it's not like me that.

We ask a bloke where the nearest Tesco is he points us in the direction and tells us it is about a five minute walk. I ask all the lads to give me £25 each, they ask why and I tell them to trust me and hand it over, they give to me and I hand it to Kane.

"Here you go pal, here is a few quid to put in your pocket until we start knocking out the weed. There are a few snide sports shops like the ones on Bury New Road we saw last night."

"Here is £40 quid off me why don't you get a tracky as well so you look smart, it will go well for when we are trying to knock the gear out to locals and the people who have come here on the hen and stag parties."

"Orr safe boys, I really appreciate it yo, you know me Vinnie I can sell ice to the Eskimos and I will be knocking the skunk out like ice creams on Blackpool front Yo."

I can see the Tesco sign ahead, I am craving for a bit of the rock, I smoke the rest of the joint and promise myself a quick hit of the rock in the disabled toilets in Tesco.

George is carrying a pierced can around with him I take it off him and go into the toilet. Before I get there I see two security guards standing over there podium station clock us, they cannot hide their concern. I put them at ease by approaching them and ask where the mobile phone shop is. This is my way of saying I know you are gonna be watching us you fuckers, but I am letting you know we are not arsed! I tell the boys to go to the shop and see what basher phones they have. These are none smart phones. They do not have a GPS on them which means if any shit goes down and it goes to court they cannot pin point your phone, only relate it to the nearest mast.

"Find out what the deals are on pay as you go and get Mo a nice one too, with a camera." I laugh as I shout this to Ricky across Tesco. I notice people are looking at me but I do not give a fuck, I never have never will.

I come out of the toilet feeling even better than I did before, my message to the world of drug users right now is, if you have never mixed spice with crack cocaine you have not been high yet. I feel like I can beat every man, resolve any problem, and settle any dispute and most of all... get a cracking deal off this sales lad in the phone shop!

7

A Pub Crawl With The Locals

Ricky

Vinnie has sorted all the contracts out and is on a full mission to the Wetherspoons on the front. I am all for a day on the beer so is Kane, but George and Mo want to get off and do their own thing for a bit. We visit the head shop to buy some more spice.

"Alright fellas, good to see ya. What can I get ya?"

"I want three bags of that spice artic pal."

I am not too keen on this lad speaking to us with that much familiarity, he does not know us and I don't like to be judged by anyone, he does not know me and my suspicions are he thinks I am some low-life prick. Vinnie can see my face change; he looks at me and shakes his head, and implies me to chill.

George and Mo pay for the spice, there is another lad in the shop who I am guessing is from the area, he's buying some magic. I have had it a few times, it is lethal and keeps you up for days, miles better than any overpriced bashed up cocaine from some prick of a drug dealer who is probably three ranks down from someone like Dermo.

"I Will have a bag of that too pal," I think 'fuck it why not'. Beer and spice is not the best combo so it will keep me going, plus the way we have been tanning the rock, it won't last forever. George and Mo get a bag to share too, not that George ever needs prompting to take a drug; it's like prompting a veggie to go for the salad in a steak house!

"Alright boys I will call you both later, we will be in one of the pubs round here. See you laters."

Vinnie has a word with them both too. "Listen, you crazy fuckers don't be going wild on that magic and robbing the shops; if we get nicked we have a lot to lose, box clever boys."

Mo and George leave towards the tower and have a look that says we will rob whatever we want, which I am sure is their plan. George cannot go into any Tesco without taking something; he even came out with a sandwich before then threw it away when nobody wanted to eat it, a thieving cunt if I ever knew one. We bounce towards the Wetherspoons, I am thinking I hope they both get nicked and slammed or drown in the sea as they are out of the deal.

The pub looks busy, as there are around ten people outside smoking and I always think you can judge the numbers inside on how many there are outside, plus it is the August Bank Holiday Monday; the last of the year so it is going to be busy anyway. Kane goes to the bar to get the beers in, I go to the toilet to snort a key of the magic, let's see what I have been missing. I walk into the toilet straight into the cubicle; I can hear someone in the cubicle next to me sniffing a line of what I presume to be coke, a fucking waste of money if you ask me, better off with the rock and spice than the weed and the coke. I put a small mountain of the magic on my key, it is actually the key to the safe in the B&B where the skunk awaits us to bag up and sell, an inner devil inside me makes me contemplate leaving here and going back, taking the bag and fucking off from these, I won't just yet, but the devil is calling. I snort the powder PHOAH! It hits me in an instant, it like a rush from speed, but a high from cocaine.

"You fucking beauty," I say out loud.

I walk out in to the bar to see Vinnie and Kane sat outside with a refreshing pint for me... Fuck me I am wired! I take a gulp of my pint before I sit down; raise the glass to Kane and Vinnie.

"Cheers boys, to what I think is going to be a wild day in Blackpool."

"Have you just had some of the magic bro?" Kane asks me.

"Yeah it's fucking top. I'm on the ceiling."

"Give us go of it then, bro."

I pass him the gear and the safe key and he is off to the toilets handing me a joint of spice he has just rolled.

Vinnie drops his voice a little, for probably the first time in history, "listen I will talk to you about the chopping up of the weed in a bit and how we will have a little side earner okay, pal?"

"Yeah, safe," I tell him I have had a few ideas too. I am about to tell him my plans when Kane comes out of the toilet looking like he has just been hit with a bolt of lightning.

"Told you it was strong." I say to him.

Kane is laughing, I know how he feels. Vinnie takes the safe key off Kane and goes to the bar; he comes back with two plastic cocktail stirrers he passes one each to me and Kane.

"Snap the end of the stirrer off and keep this in your pocket. If this key keeps getting passed about we will end up losing it and that is the last thing we want." I know that Vinnie is just getting paranoid and is worried that one of us will do a runner with it.

We have a few more beers in the Wetherspoons then go into the Manchester pub. It is full of gangs of lads from different areas and we don't like the vibe. We decide to have a quick beer, a key of magic then go; we are not arsed about the company in fact, in the next few days we will be glad of it.

We hit a couple of the pubs just off the back streets, we have gone off the pints and on to the Jack Daniels and coke, and they do some good deals in Blackpool on the shorts. The beer is great and all but I get a bit bloated with it so it's better to change, for one thing, I am not drunk, well I don't feel it anyway. I feel on top form but at the same time I know by body is exhausted.

I get a text from George, "WHER r UZ". I cannot be arsed with all that texting so I just call him.

"Where are you pal?" He tells me that they are on the North Pier in the arcades and ask us to come down.

"Okay pal we will be down that way in an hour or so, we are just having another beer. George is fucked off his face and telling me about the homeless lads he has been speaking to."

"You're breaking up pal, I will call you back." I put the phone down.

"Those two are both wired," I tell Kane and Vinnie. Kane looks back at me, he is going grey.

"You okay, pal?"

"Nah Bro, I am feeling bad Yo, think I need to lie down."

Vinnie bursts out laughing at him.

"You soft fucker, you have only had about four pints."

With that, Kane empties his stomach under the table, it smells bad. No one has noticed yet, we get up and go. As soon as the fresh air hits us Kane throws up again. His legs are going weak and I can see he is not in a good way. We hold him up until he can sort himself out and decide we better get him back to the B&B to sleep it off. He can take his drugs with no issues this lad but a few pints and a couple of shots, he is fucked up. We take him back to the B&B and leave him on the camper bed. Vinnie sets up two pieces of rock and we have a good go of it before we go back out.

8

Vida Street

George

Me and Mo have been mooching about in the arcades and around the area all day. We spent a couple of hours on a bike game – it was top. The Tower was £35 to go up but we did not pay and got up there for nothing. I got caught nicking a key ring out of the souvenir shop at the top so the security threw us both out. I am not arsed anyway, at least we got up there and did not have to pay. There are loads of homeless people here in Blackpool and we have been chatting to a lad called Ray and his bird Toni. They have told us that everyone goes to Vida Street. It is a place for young homeless and rough sleepers in Blackpool. There are all sorts of support there; I guess it is like the YPSF. We went there with them but it was locked. Ray tells me that they can sort me out with accommodation here because I was in care just like him, even though I do not have a connection to the area.

We smoke a few joints of spice together and he introduces us to some of the street homeless beggars. You can earn good money begging at the weekends and especially today, through the week in the holiday season is good but other than that you are better off going into a city like Manchester and Liverpool. Ray is on heroin and so is his girlfriend, he also injects magic as well as heroin; he says it is the cleanest way to take it. I am not into needles and stuff I tell him. We go and chill on the square which is on the main area of Blackpool's front. It has concrete benches, there is a few lads there who are all homeless or in hostels, it's where they all hang out together and get drunk and wrecked once they have earned their money for the day begging.

We walk over with Ray and I see a lad form Manchester I know, Joel.

"No way pal, how are you doing bro, when did you get up here?"

"How are you, George, and how are you little Mo?"

"I am sound bro," I tell him. "How long have you been up here like?"

Joel tells me he has been here a couple of weeks with Dessie and another lad who I do not know called Tommo. Mo is looking at me with a straight face which says something is wrong. I know what it is straight away; the lad Dessie is the one that Ricky battered a while back. I wink at Mo and let him know I'm obviously on the ball.

"Who are you here with?"

"Just us two pal. Lee took us to Blackpool and we decided to stay for a bit."

"Are you on the street then?"

"Yeah pal, where are you crashing?" I ask straight away.

"We have a squat that is an old B&B that will be getting refurbished, so we are crashing there at the minute; do you want to come there tonight?"

I am put on the spot by him, so I just say yeah, but we are gonna have a mooch around for a bit first.

His pal, Dessie comes over and says hello; he is a sound lad and offers us some of his joint. He tells us he has been in a bad way with the spice and was in hospital up here not too long ago with bad chest pains and strong pains all over his body. He tells me there is word that there may be a detox programme opening in Blackpool according to the workers at Vida Street. We tell him we have got to get off and say we will catch back up later. Just before we go Dessie asks me if I have seen "that fucker Ricky". I tell him I have not seen him and go.

9

It Gets Messy

Vinnie

George and Mo have now phoned me telling us to meet them; we agree to meet back at the Wetherspoons. The situation is good right now as Kane is in bed; those two will take a while to meet up so I can finally talk shop with Ricky.

"Okay pal, this is the plan I have for the sell. Kane, Mo and George can sell to the locals and the tourists by hanging about on the front near the pubs arcades and wherever the homeless get together, which is probably our B&B," I laugh as I say this, but quickly get myself together, this is business.

"We will knock out £20 bags weighing 3.5 grams, an eighth that's eight bags to an ounce having a return of £160. There are just over 35 ounces in a kilo, call it 35, meaning our return on a kilo will be £5600.00 times that by 2 is £11,200, less around a grand for expenses and living cost. We will obviously have to explain this to them three as they will eventually figure it out, however I will do the weighing on the scales with you and we will just put 3 gram into each bag giving us a remaining 4 gram on each ounce that will give us and extra 280 grams they are not aware about we will bag that up into 93 extra bags giving us an extra £1860.00 which is £930.00 extra for me and you."

"Sounds good to me Vinnie, you're a shrewd lad when it comes to trade I will give you that, what if someone asks for an ounce or half ounce?"

Vinnie rapidly responds like he has already thought of this situation, "We tell them to fuck right off, you get 2 gram for £20 up here and we will be knocking the £20 bags out like it is giving Christmas turkeys to the poor. These fuckers from Blackpool will be all over us, I won't be surprised if a local lad is working for us within a week, and if things need to change we will change them, but trust me pal. This is the golden egg potentially we can make good dough here and all we have to do is sit in a pub, smoke spice, drink beer eat take away while the spice boys are running around Blackpool bringing in the monies. The good thing is we will only give em 10 bags at a time so Mo can keep running back to us for more and we can keep going back to the B&B when we get low on bags."

"It sounds like a good plan to me Vinnie, Cheers" Ricky and Vinnie raise their glasses and both finish the rest of their pint in one gulp and leave the pub.

Mo and George meet us outside the Wetherspoons. We go in together and start to chase the pints with Jaeger bombs, we are all high as fuck on a mixture of crack, Magic, spice and alcohol... this is probably the last thing I remember about the night as it went a bit hazy after this.

10

Tattoo

Vinnie

I wake up to the smell of sick, fart and sweat, the room is spinning and I have a thirst like never before. Mo, Kane and George are all in the double bed, Kane's clothes are on the camp bed covered in sick and Ricky is on the floor with his shoes still on his feet. The last thing I remember was being thrown out of a pub because Ricky arguing with a landlord for smoking spice, the rest really is a BLACKOUT!

"Ricky, Ricky," I call out, he lifts his head, and looks at me. "What time did we get in?"

"I don't know, I cannot remember Vin," he replies.

The others come round, Kane still looks rough.

"Yo boys I am rough you know, them spirits fucked me up, I am sticking to the beer and drugs, fuck that, let us look at your tattoos again yo."

"What?" I say.

"Your tattoos you all had 'em done last night."

"YOU'RE FUCKING JOKING ME!"

"No, bro check your chest out, you all got the same."

I look on my chest and see it! In funny writing I see it on my fucking chest:

THE SPICE BOYS

"WHAT THE FUCCCKKKK!" I shout out, waking up everyone. "Take your tops off boys." The lads lift up their t-shirts and it's there for all to see:

THE SPICE BOYS

on the left side of our chest above our nipples where you would have a logo on a t-shirt. Mo has a Nike swoosh sign under his spice boys tattoo. Ricky has also had a Lacoste crocodile tattooed on the other side of his chest as well as the spice boy's. George does not seem to have anything else other than the "spice boys" and then it gets worse.

"Have you checked out the one on your back?"

"WHAT'S ON MY BACK?" I say to Mo. "WHAT THE FUCK. **RIP DAD 2/03/2015.**" I cannot believe it, what is worse is that he died on the 4th not the 2nd – the 2nd is my sister's birthday! Holy shit. I have to smile though when George gets up and I see a Yin Yang tattoo on the back of his left side shoulder.

"What the fuck have you had that done for?" George just shakes his head and builds a joint.

"I am never having that magic again and this shit tattoo is getting covered as soon as I can."

"You was asking to have rosary beads around your neck at first but the guy said he could not finish it in one session, you said you was not arsed and would come back to have it done."

"Mo, why did you not stop me mate?"

"I don't mind it and it was your suggestion mate you said this would bond us all together for life."

"Next time I come up with shit like that knock me out." Vinnie feels like he is going into shock.

Ricky has his head in his hands and I can hear him mumbling to himself in shock looking down at the crocodile on his chest; he is actually trying to rub it off, I have never seen him this quiet before.

"Should I burn it off with a cig?" he says to us all.

"No pal, we will just have to get it covered with something this week."

"I know this," he says," I am not going back to Manchester until we have got these off us, we will be the laughing stock of the city."

11

Court Room Eight

Janey

They take me up from the cells first thing in the morning. I have cold sweats and was convulsing during the night. I get to speak with my solicitor who advises me to go guilty on the common assault charge, he will mitigate that I was mocked and goaded due to me being homeless by the lads and I have reacted. I am also looking at a ban from entering the gardens due to my so-called aggressive begging and I will probably be fined and have to pay court costs.

I am feeling really sick and I just want to get out of here; it has been three days since I was locked up due to the bastard Bank Holiday Monday. I nod to my solicitor, I have no fight in me whatsoever and I have pains in my arms stomach and legs, I just want this to be over. My solicitor leaves and I go to my cell only to be called up to Court Room Eight ten minutes later. I am shaking as I go into the dock. The magistrate can see this but shows not a single bit of emotion towards me. He asks me to give my name, date of birth and address, which is no fixed abode. I look to the gallery and I see Lee, a sense of relief is over me as I know he will wait for me and help me out when I am released. The magistrate asks for my plea. I tell him guilty, he wastes no time in commenting on the number of young people in the centre of Manchester intimidating the public with aggression for money to feed their drug habits. I can feel myself going faint and just want him to finish and let me go back to the camp.

I hear him sentence me to six months suspended sentence with court cost of £250.00 as well as £200.00 compensation to the victim and a four month ban from entering the Piccadilly Gardens. He was going to give me a city centre ban, but I have to access probation and I need to use the YPSF service to get accommodation. As I am being sent down to the cells to meet my solicitor he tells me that if he sees me in the court room again he will not hesitate to lift my suspended sentence.

My solicitor says the sentence was a bit harsh and has concerns on how I am going to pay the fine as I am not in receipt of benefits. I sign the sheet and leave the cells without thanking him as I could have done better myself.

Lee is waiting outside for me with that stupid "concerned" look he has!

"How are you Janey, would you like to come and have a brew and something to eat?"

I nod back at him.

"They have had me in there since Saturday; it's a fucking piss take," I tell him. "Have you got a cig?"

"No, I do not smoke," he replies.

I walk over to a young lad and girl who are outside the court.

"Hiya, have ya got a spare cig please? I have just got out and have been locked up for three days." They look at me and have no issues passing me a cig.

"They're fuckers aren't they, my dad has been in since Saturday too, we 'ave not been able to see him or anything."

"Orr nice one, I hope you dad gets out, cheers."

I walk back to Lee who looks like he is about to lecture me on begging, but I can see he thinks twice. We go to a nice coffee shop just near the town hall, it's a bit posh and I can see them staring at me, so does Lee who is pretty good in these situations.

"You alright, love!" Lee says in a firm thick Mancunian dialect. The woman smiles and puts her head down. That is something I have noticed about Lee and his lot, they will stand up to people who judge us by our appearance and make them feel like outcast.

"Are you going to come to the YPSF with me to get yourself on the list to be accommodated, Janey? You have been rough sleeping for too long now and really need to get yourself into accommodation and cleaned up. I really worry for your physical and mental health."

"I will but I need to see Ricky first, he has been away all weekend, he left me at the drop in and I have not seen him since."

"He is in Blackpool, Janey, he has stayed there with Kane, Mo, George and Vinnie."

"OH FUCKING HAS HE, THE BASTARD!" I break into tears, my stomach and bones are aching. I tell Lee I will meet him at the YPSF at one o'clock today. I have to go and make some money first and I will need to go to Elysium. I finish my breakfast and leave, he asks me to go with him again but he knows I am not coming. I need a hit and I need some money.

I walk up towards Chinatown then cross Portland Street on to the back of the gay village. I have not had to do this alone for a while and I am a bit scared, it is early in the day but there is always someone within thirty minutes in the centre who is looking for sex. It is easy to do it when you're high or have been on a run of a few nights, but for me, I am not a prostitute, I will fuck someone for money in desperate circumstances. Sex means nothing to me. I have had sex with loads of people since I was thirteen, it is worthless to me. I want some money and if someone is willing to part with their money for twenty minutes in their car so be it. I wait for five minutes and a middle aged man pulls over in a white van.

12

Old Foes

Kane

Vinnie and Ricky are going to start bagging up the weed today. They have gone to buy some scales and we have been told to go to the Vida Street drop in to check out how many people are using the place and see what the score is.

My job is to speak with the people in there and see if they want any weed while George is going to register himself homeless and see what accommodation they can offer him. Mo is not going to register himself as he is not too sure if he is reported missing and does not want to get nicked and sent back to Manchester.

Vida Street is in a residential street less than half a mile from where we are staying in the South Shore. It looks like it is two old houses knocked together yet it is refurbished with clean colours of pale blue and cream and it looks more modern than the YPSF and has a pool table and some games stuff, it reminds me of one of the old type youth clubs when we go in.

I am just gonna front it with the boys in there and give it the big one like a true south Manc G! A woman approaches us and says hello and asks are we here to present as homeless.

"I am not but he is, I am here to check it out, Yo is that okay?"

"Yes of course, my name is Mandy and the drop in is open three mornings a week. Get yourselves a drink and have a game of pool. The service is here for you when you need it. We do ask that you sign in first."

I sign in and walk over to get a brew. And hear a voice call me.

"Yes Kane, what are you doing here?" It is Joel and his mate Dessie with a couple of other lads, who I guess are homeless and have the look of someone who loves the spice.

"Yo safe boys, what you saying?"

"We saw them two last night how come you are here?"

I tell him about the trip with Lee and that we decided to stay, .Joel tells me that he came with Dessie who was up here a few years ago when he was in care. "We had enough of Manchester and needed a break. I am wanted for something up there as well so it was best to get out of the way for a bit."

Joel tells Kane, "I was on the streets for a bit, there is a big community up here of young and old people, but I got accommodated once I came here. We are officially staying in a hostel nearby which is okay but we also have a squat at a B&B, it is better up here, the job centre go a bit easier on you if you're not on the sick but are homeless."

I tell them I am making a joint and do they want to come out for a smoke. I have a cheeky key of the magic in the bogs to put my confidence high and come out with the rolled joint.

"Yes boys, let's go and blaze this bad boy, it's strong shit going about at the minute Yo."

"I am telling you, it is always stronger up here, that fucker Jazz was probably ripping us all off says Joel."

They don't ask me if Ricky is with me but something tells me they already know. I also know that they spoke with Mo and George last night. I chat a bit about Manchester and what's been going on at the camps and stuff as well as get the info off them about where everyone hangs out who is on the streets in Blackpool. The best information I get from them is about the pubs and the choice of drugs. Magic and spice are big in Blackpool but there is a load of people who still love skunk weed in the tent community, which is smaller than Manchester's as everyone can get in a bed and breakfast up here. He rolls off a few names of the B&BS and ours comes up in the list, I just about hide my smirk from them, Vinnie will be fuming!

George comes out with Mo; he has to come back tomorrow. His new worker will try and accommodate him, she can get him in an emergency bed tonight, if he can come back at four p.m. to see if there is a bed available but he told her he has a fear of sharing rooms with other people since he was attacked at the Steelfort court emergency accommodation a while back. She said that for now he will have to wait until he has been properly processed with the council and listed as an official rough sleeper.

"We are getting off, yo; we will catch up with youze later if you are about?"

"Yeah safe, see you later, bro."

We walk back towards the South Shore without looking back.

"I don't trust them shady fuckers, something is not right, yo."

"What was they saying to you, Kane," asks Mo.

"Nothing bro, it is what they did not say, that Dessie guy is a shady fucker and I knew it when I saw him in the YPSF a while ago, watch that one I am telling you both, yo."

I ring Ricky and tell him who I have been talking to, he is not a bit bothered and he tells me he will just put it on him again if the cunt starts. I leave it at that I tell them we are on our way back and he ask us to go to the head shop and buy some more snap bags.

13

Black Street Boys

Vinnie

We get some scales from a local food store, I am getting
excited now, I can feel the nerves kicking in and I am
singing Blackstreet's "*No Diggity*" over and over in my
head. The song obviously means something different to
our means, but I am feeling good right now, high as a
kite and not even the tattoos from hell can keep me
down. I think we will bag up thirty bags for a start and
see how long it takes us to knock it out to the locals and
tourists.

I am going to send Kane on to the front today and
see if it is worth investing in a daily Pleasure Beach pass
from one of the local workers who we seen in the pub
the other night, there has to be a scam on somewhere to
get into that place. There are coach loads of students,
youth clubs and community groups that go into there
every day and we have the market while it is here. In the
evenings we can have the boys mooching up the front
asking lads and girls going into bars if they need any
weed and we also need to get in with the locals but my

thoughts are once they hear that you get an eighth for £20 we'll be in business.

Ricky's phone goes off and I can see his chest rise, "is that right, fuck 'em like I say, I will put it on the ginger twat as soon as I see him if he wants what I give him last time again he can have it. Meet us back at the B&B in about an hour and half we have got to sort something first."

"Hey Vinnie, that Dessie and Joel are here, I am gonna give it him pal."

I advise Ricky to leave it and see if we can use them to hook us up with the connections, let's see if we can take them for a couple of beers later and work it from there, if they don't want to know then fuck him up, simples! Ricky contemplates this as we walk past the head shop on our way back to the B&B I see a notice on the door.

The Psychoactive Substance Act
What is it? The Psychoactive Substances Act (PSA) comes into force on 26th October 2015

1. The Act makes it an offence to produce, supply or offer to supply any psychoactive substance if the substance is likely to be used for its psychoactive effects and regardless of its potential for harm.

The only exemption to the PSA is those substances already controlled by the Misuse of Drugs Act, nicotine, alcohol, caffeine and medicinal products. The main intention of the PSA is to shut down shops and websites that currently trade in 'legal highs'. Put simply, any substance is illegal to produce or supply if it is likely to be used to get high.

Introduction of the Act: The Bill was given Royal Assent on the 28th January 2015 and was due to start on 6th April 2015 although this was delayed until 26th October 2015.

Existing laws: The PSA doesn't replace the Misuse of Drugs Act (1971) so laws around existing illegal (controlled) drugs will remain the same. Temporary Class Drug Orders (TCDOs) can still be applied and the Human Medicines Regulations (2012) will remain the same. However the

Intoxicating Substances Supply Act (1985)* will be scrapped.

At present, a substance causing concern must be reviewed by the ACMD (the Advisory Council on the Misuse of Drugs) to assess any potential harm. The ACMD then advise the government on a course of action. The government do not have to take this advice, but are bound to consult the ACMD first. The ACMD will still have a role and a 'new' or emerging psychoactive substance can still be brought under the Misuse of Drugs Act, but the PSA was introduced without consulting the ACMD and fundamentally changes UK drug legislation.

Possession: Possession of a psychoactive substance **is not an offence**, except in a 'custodial institution' (prison, young offender centre, removal centre etc.). The definition of custodial institution does not include Mental Health secure units. 4 Possession with intent to supply, importing or exporting a psychoactive substance are all offences under the PSA.

Importation: The PSA does not include possession as an offence as the government did not want it to lead to the mass criminalisation of young people. It has however been pointed out by some commentators that the importing of a psychoactive substance would include buying a psychoactive substance from a non-UK based website, which may lead to individuals being prosecuted.

Supply and production: The main thrust of the PSA is intended to act against shops and websites supplying 'legal highs'. If the experience of similar legislation introduced in Ireland is repeated the visible outlets selling them will most likely disappear. The PSA is also quite specific in that the onus is on the sellers and producers of a substance to ensure it is not 'likely' to be consumed for its psychoactive effects.

Penalties under the Psychoactive Substances Act 2015:
Offence Summary
(Magistrates Court)
Indictment
(Crown Court)
Possession **Not an offence**
Possession in a custodial institution Up to 12 months and/or a fine* Up to 2 years and/or a fine Possession with intent to supply Up to 12 months and/or a fine* Up to 7 years and/or a fine Supply/offer to supply etc. Up to 12 months and/or a fine* Up to 7 years and/or a fine

Production Up to 12 months and/or a fine* Up to 7 years and/or a fine

Importation/exportation Up to 12 months and/or a fine* Up to 7 years and/or a fine

Failure to comply with a Prohibition or Premises notice Up to 12 months and/or a fine* Up to 2 years and/or a fine

*Summary convictions in Northern Ireland are up to 6 months and/or a fine.

Offences under the PSA would be considered 'aggravated' if they involved supply to under 18s, were near a school or a children's home (Local authority children's homes etc.).

Powers of stop and search: Police will have powers of stopping and searching individuals and premises, however possession of psychoactive substances will not be an offence and which substances are actually psychoactive is far from legally clear at present. 5 Currently the Association of Chief Police Officers (now the National Police Chiefs' Council) guidance states that a 'legal high' should be treated like a controlled drug until proven otherwise. Further guidance may be issued.

Premises and Prohibition notices: Within the PSA there are quite detailed powers given to the police and local authorities for dealing with the licensees (owners etc.) of shops and UK-based websites, and penalties for failure to comply with notices issued under this section of the PSA.

Definition of psychoactive: Quite what constitutes a psychoactive substance is one of the most contentious issues in the Act, which defines it as: *"any substance which (a) is capable of producing a psychoactive effect in a person who consumes it, and (b) is not an exempted substance".* The government are confident that a psychoactive substance can be defined, tested simply and cost effectively and subsequently proven. The ACMD among others have argued consistently that the definition used is too broad and is unworkable in practice. The Home Secretary responded to the concerns of the ACMD in November 2015.

Exemptions: Nicotine, alcohol and caffeine will be exempt from being classed as psychoactive substances. Medicinal products as defined by the Human Medicines Regulations (2012) and drugs already controlled by the Misuse of Drugs Act (1971) will also be exempt. Further exemptions can be made by the Secretary of State after consultation with the ACMD.

We just look at each other and walk into the shop. There are four other lads in there with concerned faces that look like they have just had their benefits stopped and their employment coach has just told them they have been given a twelve hour a day job shit shifting!

"Jay, what does that mean in the window, is it bollocks pal?" I say with desperation in my voice that I was not expecting.

"It means I am out of a job in two months! The council and the police came in this morning and told me I would be stripped of my traders licence if I do not make everyone aware as from today. The government have to give two months' prior notice once a substance ban has been passed apparently."

"Fucking hell," I say, "what you gonna do?"

Ricky jumps in, "What are we gonna do? I am not ready for this I really am not, fuck me man this is bad, is it everywhere or just Blackpool?" he asks in hope.

"Everywhere pal, fucking everywhere!"

With this, Ricky buys three bags of spice and some more magic as the rock is dwindling away to just a few pebbles now. We head off to the B&B; I tell the lads in the shop that we have eighths of skunk for £20 if they want any. I give them Kane's number and tell them they can call it 24/7; someone will always answer. No time like the present to get things going.

I have just levelled the price of skunk weed with spice. I am sure spice will be surging in price in the next week or so, considering these factors I am currently in the right market. I think to myself had I been born into money I would probably be working on the stock market in London now, I curse myself sometimes for not having the good sense to be born into an upper middle class family in the south.

I am no longer singing *Bag It Up* in my head, *The End* by The Doors is playing now. I think it is time to get wrecked on beer and drugs as soon as I take care of business and send the boys out to graft.

We make our way back to the B&B and I begin to notice that not only can I pick out the homeless people and put them all into categories, they can see it in me and the boys too. We must have passed about twenty beggars in the last two days and not one of them have said "can you spare some change please" to us. Yet I hear them call it out to every person or family walking ahead of us and behind us. This, I say to myself will change; the homeless spice addict vibe we give off will be coming to an end for me soon. The profits of this business are going to be mine added with the claim from the council. I am about to start my exit plan and get back into society: a car, a job, a girl, a home with a flat screen telly, laminate floor, a washer dryer and neighbours who look out for you. Drinking in the Northern Quarter and going out for meals! Fuck this life I am existing in, now is the time to strike and leave these behind and never return and I look forward to the day when I will be asked to "spare some change".

I walk in to the B&B which is clear now that it is nothing more than an emergency hostel for homeless. Pickwick is just hoping to catch the odd holidaymaker who has not had the good sense to look at TripAdvisor for reviews, I can picture a father who has stayed here with their family thinking "fuck me if we would have only read a Trip Advisor review in advance".

I bag up thirty bags just before Mo, George and Kane come back in. Kane is fucked off his face, they all are! Ricky is questioning Kane about Dessie and Joel. Something tells me he is worried about them two. I am not though; I will smash fuck out of them both and their backward coastal mates!

I explain the bags, the cut and the price as well as our return. They all seem happy and to be honest, it goes over their thick skulls; all they know is we split it five ways and they want £2000 each when all is sold.

"Me and Ricky are going into the local pubs and will be buying beers and befriending anyone in a Pleasure Beach t-shirt that is having a pint after their shift. We want a free Pleasure Beach passes in exchange for weed ideally but I will be happy to give cash. Mo and George can be on the front with Kane. Kane can approach people on the front; the tourist, couples, stag parties, the kids and anyone else who you think passes for a smoker."

"Mo, George keep an eye on Kane and look out for the coppers etc. Don't be chatting to each other every two minutes. Keep your eyes peeled for coppers and ring us if you have any issues. We can meet up back here about three a.m. or when it goes quiet. Don't forget at weekends that night club is open until four a.m. and they will want nothing more than a bag of weed to come down with after they have been on their uppers."

I hand ten bags to each of them and split the last of the crack cocaine with them.

"Enjoy the last of the rocks boys, after this it is just magic and spice to keep you going… lay off the spice a bit too while you're working, don't be fucking keeling over wasted because you have over done it."

I am hoping the thirty bags go and we get a £600 return. Within the next month or so, we will have to sell 666 bags to get rid of the lot it should be 571 bags at 3.5g but the bags are only 3g due to me and Ricky's side earner. I reckon we can rid of forty bags a day with the tourist and locals, but I think we should double the sales over the weekend with a realistic target of one hundred bags for Friday Saturday and Sunday.

14

Second Nature

Kane

I have been selling drugs since I was about ten years old. I used to just do a few runs for my step dad on my bike. The selling bit is easy for me Yo, it's the money and the drugs I cannot control, it's where things go wrong for me. If I am honest, I like drugs a lot, but I enjoy spending money with a gal, taking her out and spoiling her, it feels good to have a nice gal on your arm. My step dad used to tell me that the girls I lie down with are no good, he would say 'Kane if you lie down with dogs you come up with fleas!' Or chlamydia in my case, several times in fact. I might stay up here if things are okay or at least for the rest of the good weather, there will be money to be made and honeys to entertain. Blackpool make way for Kaneyay.

On this front it is easy to sell. I knocked three bags out in five minutes to some lads wearing Burnley FC tops; football tops are basically a sign to me that says will exchange money for drugs. I am wearing a t-shirt that says 'I heart (love) Blackpool' that I bought from the shop on the front for a fiver. I was sick over my other top so I have this for now. I look like an idiot in it but it does not attract too much attention so I'm not arsed. I tried to sell a weed to the lad who was begging but he was more interested in my joint of spice, so I gave him the last bit. First rule of selling drugs, keep the locals happy as they will be the first to turn on you! I have sent George across the road directly opposite me. I have an eye on him and he can see me. I also have Mo walking up and down both sides for the front. He has the biggest candy floss you can buy in one hand and joint of spice in the other so he is happy as he can be.

I used to sell heroin in Nottingham a few years back and I was earning £160.00 a day, it was easy money a gang of five sellers and my cousin and his pal was the brawn of the operation and supplied us with the wraps of gear. We had a couple of run in's with the locals, but nothing too big. One of my pals is still living down there with a girl he met he has had a couple of kids too. Another two of my pals have just been released from the prison down there as we all got lifted by the feds, yo. I only had money on me and the surveillance team watching us never actually got any concrete evidence on me so I got off clean with no further action.

I see three lads coming towards me with cans of Fosters in their hands.

"Yes boys, do you want to buy any bud?"

"How much is it mate?" The tallest of the three ask in a thick Scouse accent.

"£20 bags for an eighth."

"Go ed then lah, I will have one let's see it, like."

I hold the bag in my hand, he goes out to take it, but I am too wise in the game.

243

"Money first boys, you know the script!"

The lad laughs and passes me the £20. "You got to try lad," and winks.

"Where are you from pal, Manchesda?"

"Nah, I'm from Bolton," I say, but unlike the weed he is not buying it that I am from Bolton he knows I am a Manc like I know he's a scouser. He smells the weed and I can see by his face he likes what he's bought. I give him my number and tell him to call me if he wants any more.

15

Social Networking

Vinnie

The pubs are busy in the back streets. I notice the locals have a card that gives them a discount on the beer. I have to get one of them. Ricky has come back around a bit and is high off the last bits of crack we have left. His lips, like mine, are chapped and dry through the burn of the rock when it hits your lips. I start talking to a guy from the Pleasure Beach that is sat with another lad from the area; his bright orange Blackpool FC top gives this away.

"Are you from round here lads?" I ask.

"I am from Fleetwood originally but I live here now. I work on the Pleasure Beach," he says with pride.

I look at the big Blackpool Pleasure Beach sign on his polo shirt and want to say "oh I just thought you had bought that shirt to wear for going out like" but I will save my humour for people who understand it. I don't think this coastal clown is a full bob which is exactly the kind of prey I am looking to manipulate. He introduces himself as Simon and his football jersey wearing pal as Michael.

"What team do you support?" Michael asks me and Ricky.

"We don't like football mate," Vinnie tells the boys, this is enough to cut the football conversation off straight away. Vinnie thinks to himself, I suppose I am a City fan , but I'm not really into football or can I ever be interested in discussing a load of multi-millionaires who don't even look at me or my kin when they pass us in the posh Spinningfields area of the city. The footballers are the best at not seeing anything around them but aware of everyone watching them. Ricky Hatton, on the other hand is sound, he always gives us a score and will chat for five minutes or so but it is usually about football!

Ricky starts to talk about where he is from and other shite whilst I get the beers in, which impresses the lads as Michael's hand is outstretched before the pint hits the table. I quickly turn the conversation to drugs, skunk specifically and I am happy to know both of them like a smoke. I pass them a bag and ask them to skin up in the bogs then we can have a smoke when we go to the next pub together.

"Why don't you lads show us the other side of Blackpool, where the locals drink, we would rather be there than in the tourist trap of Wetherspoons and the Manchester pub; we will get the beers in lads."

Michael and Simon look at each other like their numbers have come in on the lottery and I have to ask myself how far is the gap between homelessness and working with a fixed abode is in this part of the world as these two don't really convince me to go back into society if they can be so easily bought. I offer to buy a couple of bottles of beer to gulp down whilst waiting for the joint to be rolled. Simon hands me his "locals discount card" which I assure you he won't be seeing again.

We hit a couple of pubs and are all pissed up, only the magic is separating us from the Blackpool lads who are intent on telling us their life stories. I am making all the right noises, agreeing and nodding and raising my glass to look like I actually give a fuck!

It's not too long before they start bitching about their job, the low pay and the Eastern Europeans who have nicked the local's jobs. I have heard this shit a thousand times before, but stand loyal with them and start blaming the government, immigration and the usual shite.

"Do you think you can get hold of any wrist bands at discount price?" I ask, "We are here for a while and would want one a day, do you know anyone who could get them and we would give a good price."

"What kind of pass do you want?" Simon is clearly the one who can sort it out.

"What do you mean; they're all the same aren't they?" I ask and I admit I am a bit confused here.

"No you can pay £30 to go on all the rides or £6 a day to just enter the Pleasure Beach." FUCKING BINGO I think to myself. I thought we would have to shell out for a full pass.

"Is that right?" I say all cool hiding my delight.

Ricky has also clicked to how good this could be, we could have full access to the Pleasure Beach, sell the weed in there and on the front too.

"What would you charge us for four passes a day just to enter for the full week?" Ricky is a good wing man but deals his hand too early for me.

"I don't know you see it's my girlfriend who is on the desk and she can get them willy nilly."

I instantly exchange numbers with Simon and get another four pints, the last ones I will be buying these two I must add.

16

First Night Shift Over

Mo

We sell all the bags at around one o'clock in the morning. Kane's number went off a couple of times from lads Vinnie and Ricky had spoken to in the day. He thought it was Vinnie fucking about when it rang at first, but no, it was genuine, followed by a couple more calls through the night. I did the running for them as they was a bit away from us. It was not a problem though they were easy enough to deal with. Kane gave me his knife just in case anyone got clever and tried to rob me.

"Just stick in the top of the leg if any boy gets smart, it hurts like fuck in the thigh and stops them from running away too."

Something told me he was speaking from experience. Anyway, there was no problem. The first lot I served up was two homeless lads and a girl and the next lot just looked like gamers, they spoke less than me which was uncomfortable and at the same time comfortable as I don't really speak to people I don't know.

Kane rings Vinnie who is still in the pub, he asks us to come and meet him, but we just want to go back and have a smoke. He says he will be at the B&B in five minutes and we head back with some fish and chips and we buy some cokes too. I enjoyed tonight, seeing all the people smiling and laughing and little kids with their helium balloons, neon spinning toys and light sabres.

The street sellers who sold the toys and neon lit things could see what we were doing, but they did not show any interest or concern. I think they just saw it as we were not interfering with their trade or their customers. A big bloke who was selling near Kane even bought two bags off him and took Kane's number. It was a good night really and I almost forgot we have been paid for it as well £100 each I think, which is really good.

We have to wait a bit for them two to get back so we can get into the room. When they come back they are both pissed and talking rubbish about free passes and "conquering this backward town" as Vinnie is now calling it.

"Uz did well tonight boys, did my boys ring youse? I told you we would kick the arse out of it. The spice boys don't fuck about."

I don't really see Vinnie this drunk, it's funny to see him being giddy and happy; he usually is always thinking about stuff and cannot stop moving about. Me and George help him up the stairs and put him on to the bed, he is mumbling about orange football tops and girlfriends making no sense to me at all. We take his shoes off and leave him to crash out on the bed while we start smoking. I really would like a bit more rock as well

, we only had a bit left and finished it on the shift in the phone box. As I say this Ricky pulls out a piece with a lighter and a can. Just what the doctor ordered I think!

17

Oxford Road

Janey

I have been staying at Metrolink camp for the last three nights; it is full of new people here. I know them all; well, I know most of the faces from around town and in Piccadilly Gardens and buying from me and Ricky.

The Oxford Road camp has been removed. The bailiffs came in and took everyone out. The councillors was there saying they will offer everyone accommodation, and I think most of them are in hotels and B&Bs. The thing the council did not say is that they have housed them in the Britland Hotel at Manchester Airport well out of the way of the city and living with all the refugees that have come here. Almost everyone has left there and come back into the city centre. There are tents in Piccadilly Gardens, King Street and even under the shelters of the shops and railway arches in Castlefield. It's the council's own fault, they should have just left everyone where they was, there was no trouble and it was a good vibe. The place was a mess though; they could have brought in the cleaners from the council.

Rosie has fallen out with her fella who has also been remanded for shop lifting. We have both been working together for a couple of hours a night to get some money; we also watch each other's back so it feels a little safer. The outreach team have seen me there a couple of times but I told them I was just waiting for someone. I am not bothered anyway, I need some money I have no benefits coming in and this is easy to me. Even that Jazz from Elysium give me some free spice when I went to the shop, he was asking if I remember some guys from a while back but I did not have a clue, anyway he got to the point and we went in the back of the shop he paid me and then gave me some free magic too which I don't use much, but in the summer it seems to be a good drug to have.

Rosie comes back on to the street and has been dropped back off round the corner. She does not look too happy judging by her face.

"What's up? Are you okay?"

"Yeah I suppose, he was a fucking prick; he wanted more than we agreed and then tried to not pay me all my money the fucking prick! I saw his work's business card in the cup holder, I picked it up and said I would go to his work and tell them all about him if he did not give me my money."

"Did he pay you?"

"Yeah, £30 instead of £25; he had no change so I just took it and got out. Anyway fuck him, should we get a drink and go in the gardens see what is going on in there, maybe they have shown their faces again."

"I hope not, Rosie because the way I feel about Ricky right now is probably gonna land me in jail. I want to kill him I swear it."

We wander off into Piccadilly Gardens, the place is swarming with tents and homeless people and a new influx of drug dealers. I am aware I am not allowed in here but it will only be for half an hour tops!

18

Looked After Children

George

"George, wake up pal, you need to go to Vida Street. GEORGE WAKE UP, PAL!!"

I wake up to Vinnie shouting for me to go and sort some accommodation at the support place. He is the only human being I know that can sleep less than me. I got my head down about five this morning; we finished about one a.m. on the front then I went for a wander with Mo. I got a mobile phone out of a car door that was left unlocked and a few quid out of the drawer in the front. Mo was Clever enough to get in the boot and we now have a set of golf clubs. We stashed them and went back to collect them when we was done mooching. Vinnie was pulling his face at me about us "bringing it on top" if we get nicked but what am I supposed to do if someone leaves their car unlocked, it's not my fault, obviously I am going to take it, who wouldn't?

I go with Mo to Vida Street it is only ten a.m. and it is early for me. I usually fuck appointments off this early unless Amy or Lee pick me up take me there and drop me back off with a McDonalds. I suppose it is better to do this as we don't want to be spending into the profit and I want two thousand quid and no less. If I get the opportunity I am going to take the gear and get off with Mo I know they will do it to me if they have the chance. I would only do it with Mo like not on my own you need a mate with you when you're gonna do the dirty on your mates, but the thing is the gear and money is all mine anyway I did not have to mention it to anyone really so if anything, I am just taking my own stuff really.

The woman I spoke to is waiting for me when I get through the door. Mo goes and makes a brew and I go into her room. She has managed to track down my file from social services in Merseyside and my leaving care worker Amy in Manchester.

"Amy has asked me about your wellbeing George, she wants to know if you have a number she can contact you on."

"I don't have a phone," I tell her.

"Okay. Well I have managed to find you temporary accommodation, but we will not be able to bid on a flat for you until you have registered with Blackpool Homes. I can do that for you today and I will also start your housing benefit claim for your new accommodation, can you just sign this to say that you are okay for me to make the claim for you and start the process."

I sign the form and say nothing, I have done this hundreds of times and really don't get involved in the paperwork, that's for these people to do, I just need sorting out.

"Where am I going to be staying?" I ask.

"We have to put you in an emergency accommodation with no support, but we will be looking to put you in supported accommodation in the next month or so when a bed becomes available. The good news is that you will be given breakfast and you can come and go back to the room as you please; there is no time block when accessing the building."

"Where is it?" I ask.

"It is a nice little Bed and Breakfast quite close to the front of Blackpool so you are in a popular area..."

"Where is it?" I ask, but I know where it gonna be before the words come out of her mouth!

"It's called the South Shore Hotel, on Dickens Road about ten minutes' walk from here. The gentleman who runs it is called Mike Hardy; he is a really nice man and will be happy to help you. He knows you have the room and he will have it all cleaned and made up for you on arrival."

The bollocks these support workers feed you is unbelievable, she is making it out to be Buckingham Palace, but I know it is more like the house from the film *The Money Pitt* with Tom Hanks in it, before the work was done on it. I loved that film as a little boy, it was one of my mum's that she had on video tape and we would sometimes watch it on a Saturday afternoon with my brother when we had the flat.

"I am going to register you with the doctors and start your JSA claim for your benefits. Can you come in on Monday, the same time as today, and I can update you with everything."

"Yeah," I tell her but I will not be going. Mandy gives me £4 from the emergency homeless fund to get some lunch today. I take it off her and go.

"Come on Mo, we are going pal."

"Hi, would you like to book to see someone? Are you sleeping rough?"

"No I am okay, thank you," replies Mo as we walk out of the door.

"You won't believe this Mo. I have only been given accommodation in our hotel; fuck me how mad is that."

"Wow that is lucky; usually they put you in horrible hostels in Manchester. It really is good up here isn't it?"

I just ignore Mo and leave him in his holiday mode.

"Let's build a joint here pal then go to the head shop for some spice."

19

Fair Trades

Vinnie

Business is going really well, we have sold well over half a kilo in less than four days; I cannot believe it, Kane may be on another planet in his head but when it comes to selling drugs he really does have more front than Blackpool Beach! The golden egg was the Pleasure Beach scam. The schools and colleges are not back until next week so it was the perfect time to start selling. Michael tells me it will still stay busy through September as the Pleasure Beach will offer 50% discount tickets until October and you will see alternative members of society (my kind of people basically) who will snap up the deals throughout the week and weekends will still be mad busy too.

The deal is I can get five wristbands a day off his girlfriend Gemma – a stunning looking girl who reminds me a bit of Posh Spice – only Gemma has a few extra pounds and she has a slight cross in her left eye but still a bonny girl by no means, fuck knows how this Simon pulled her. I give them £60 at the beginning of the week and a bag of skunk and all parties are happy, well I am at least it been worth around a grand to me already.

I was thinking of taking the boys all out for a steak dinner, but then sided on the side of reality and we went to Wetherspoons. A nice restaurant would be too good for these and I don't think the restaurant would appreciate the clothes we wear, especially Kane who now has a *Simpsons* t-shirt with Homer on it with the Slogan "Can't Get Enough of that Wonderful Duff". He really does tickle me.

George has done well with the accommodation scam and has actually landed a B&B in the South Shore Hotel. The fucker has been given a single room. There are all sorts of bonuses of being a child in care; he can even have free university education if he wants, not that he will, like.

I know a lad from Nigeria who said people from his country have been using the British education system for years. Basically he came to England at sixteen, said he was fourteen, claimed asylum, stayed in school and college, was given his own flat as he was a care leaver he had a leaving care worker for three years, his driving lessons paid for and even free piano lessons that some celeb had donated money to Barnardo's for that specific reason. He is now in his last year at university and is going to be a solicitor. His mum and family have been here for the last couple of years now, as he was the youngest of the family and all the other siblings have had a middle class standard of living in care, ten times better than the one he had back home and he is a couple of years younger on his British passport too. He often tells me we have a great country.

Speaking of accommodation, it reminds me we need to renegotiate with Pickwick. This fucker has an half empty hotel, the season is over and we will not be paying anything like what we paid him a week now.

We finish our dinner and I get onto business.

"Right boys, me and Ricky will do the Pleasure Beach until seven tonight, Mo George can you do the front with Kane. When we come out I will take the mobile and do any running about tonight for the locals. It should be mad busy tonight and tomorrow right through to Sunday. If we knock all this out ahead of time we can even go on holiday somewhere."

"I don't have a passport," says Ricky.

"Don't worry about that, I will hire a car and we can go anywhere in Britain," I say trying to promote a good vibe.

"Can we stay in Blackpool?" asks Mo. I actually have no answer to that and nod as I stand up to go out for a joint.

20

All My Work

Kane

I am not happy at the long hours and standing on the front for the last five nights and inside the Pleasure Beach for the last three days selling constantly. I respect the boys have sorted me with some money for clothes but I am their sales champion. I understand Vinnie has sorted a lot of this out, but what the fuck has Ricky done to help this business venture ?! He cannot approach people and he cannot speak with new people he is a fucking liability and not doing his fair share and getting paid equal to us all. All he can do is answer the phone. Fuck him Yo.

I seen Dessie and Tommo yesterday on the front and gave them the phone number. I have not told anyone else, fuck'em. I am dealing to every punter from Edinburgh to Birmingham on this front and bringing the monies in. Let Ricky deal with Dessie, it should be interesting when he calls, which he will.

I think all the crack and magic mixed with the spice has made us all a bit shady of each other. I don't trust any of them fuckers and will take that dough and go the minute I can get my hands on the safe key. I have also bought myself a couple of pebbles of rock to keep me going while I am on the long shifts too. I was £30 short out of the funds the other day and Vinnie tried to say something, so I just come back and said that I had to split a bag up as someone complained that the three bags they bought was all underweight. The fucker did not even flinch! So I wonder what they are up to.

My phone goes off.

"Yeah boy, who is it?"

"Hiya mate it is Jack, Simon's mate from work. Do you have any weed?"

"Of course, what you after?"

"Three £20 bags."

"Yeah man, I am just near The Manchester pub outside do you want to come to meet me?"

"I will be ten minutes."

"Okay safe, Yo." I call Mo who is at The Manchester pub as I am further down. I text him the number of the caller and tell him to sort him out.

The phone goes off a few more times and I have approached around thirty people in the last two hours with a good few buyers, like I say, football tops are the best; it simply means I will exchange cash for drugs, the boys cannot say no at an offer. Easy money and it is all my work, well it's what my step dad taught me, if I am keeping it real.

21

Phone Duty

Ricky

I pick up the phone from Kane and leave him another thirty bags between him, Mo and George. We also had to pick up some more spice and magic for the boys on the front as it is going to be a long one. It has been silently agreed between us all that even though Vinnie has the key to the safe, I will be with him at all times like his shadow, this stops him from fucking off with over a kilo of weed and nearly 5K in cash.

It's weird we should all be bouncing and happy as the money is coming in, there is no heat on us from other street sellers and there does not seem to be a cop in sight, other than the odd community police officer. The thing is we all seem to be a bit suspicious of each other. I think it is because we have been tanning as many drugs as we can and mixing it with the spice which can send your head west.

I rang up a lad I know yesterday who told me that Preston has been sectioned. He was sleeping outside Boots in Piccadilly and he was singing to himself and shouting at strangers, apparently he even shit and pissed in his pants. Eventually one of the team from the YPSF seen him and what had become of him and made the call to the team at MIND who assessed him and he is now in North Manchester Hospital mental health residential unit. This is from that dirty annihilation 44, fuck me! I would not want to go out like him.

We are having a couple of beers in a pub on the back street of Blackpool called the Queen Anne chatting about the ban coming in.

"It's pretty fucking serious this mate what do you think will happen?"

"The shops will have to still sell, there is no way I can see Jazz giving up all that income and go back to just selling e-cigs and vapes. Not a chance. That firm he works with will still sell the annihilation 44 that they make in the back, but I am not smoking that shit, NO WAY. I will go back to smoking weed or fuck it all off, leave the camps, get a flat and go back to hitting the gym. This life is not forever pal. You got to have a get out plan."

I listen to Vinnie and take it all in, something tells me he is going to fuck us all, but I will be prepared for him. I know he thinks I am like them pricks, but I am not. I am one step ahead of the game every time. George, Mo and Kane will be on the streets forever, or even dead but that's not me, it carnt be, it just carnt be. The phone rings and it is a lad called Tommo asking for Kane. I tell him he is not here, but what's he after, I can sort it.

"Two £20 bags."

"No worries, meet us near the Queen Anne pub in ten minutes. I will be outside the chippy across the road."

Vinnie is on his phone talking to his sister. He has a smile on his face and I hear him tell her he will be there next week.

"Good news?" I ask him. He goes coy and says it's his niece's birthday that's all. This fucker is up to something.

I finish my pint, Vinnie gets the round in while I go and meet this lad. I see two lads approaching from the bottom of the street. I text the number to check it is them. One of the lads checks his phone, so I start to walk towards them. I recognise one on the left but I am not too sure who it is until he is right in front of me. FUCKING DESSIE! My stomach goes weak for a split second and then I decide to front it. This cunt is not phased at all, looking at his body language and something tells me he knew I would be here, but who gave him the number? I try to front it before he says anything.

"You alright, Dessie, Yeah?" I figure his reaction will be to kick off or he will play all nice. There is a short pause.

"Alright, Ricky," he says and kind of turns his back on me. That will do for me I think as I cannot be arsed with the fighting shit right now, I need to take care of business and I figure he has had his fill and wants no more. I sort out Tommo out with the weed and take the £40.

"I thought you would be on the spice, Dez?"

Dessie turns to me. "Nah man, got off it, it is for low-lives and fucks you up in the head, makes you do silly things that come back and bite ya in the arse and besides your weed prices are lower than an eighth of spice at the minute !" With this he turns and leaves with his mate. I know what he just said was a dig at me, about the bite me on the arse bit, well bring it on prick!

I walk back into the pub and the pint is on the table, but I need something stronger than the beer as I can feel a bit of anxiety kicking in with the adrenaline. I walk into the toilets and take a mighty fine big line of magic that resembles a spilling of soap powder on the work top. I hoover it up and return to Vinnie.

"What's up with you, pal?" he asks.

"That fucking lad Tommo only came with Dessie. I could not believe it, man."

"What did he say?"

"Fuck all really, he tried being a bit clever saying he was off spice as it fucks heads up and shit and that was all really."

"We could do with keeping him sweet, pal as I suspect they know people here and it could be good for business, you got to put your personal feelings aside, pal. We just want money and if they can get us the customers, well hopefully we can turn spice users to back to weed users, until our shit has gone at least. I am wired now and Vinnies way of explaining things makes sense, but I would be just happy putting the fucker in the ground if he even looks at me the wrong way again."

I go to my phone and store Tommo's number as "The cheeky fucker".

"That's fair enough Vinnie, but as the old saying goes mate, 'chat shit get banged'."

We laugh and cheers then touch our glasses together.

"Fuck it, why don't we go out to that club here tomorrow night – Dominion or something – we need a good night out I have not been to a club for ages. We can buy some jeans and a top tomorrow. Me you, Kane and if George and Mo want to come they can too, not that they will like."

We continue drinking as the phone goes off again. Business is booming.

22

A McDonald's Princess

George

It's nearly two in the morning and the McDonalds is mad busy with pissed up lads and girls falling out of the bars. Me, Mo and Kane come here after we have sold everything for something to eat, it is a good meeting point and I am always hungry in around this time, it's kind of my peak time to be awake. Obviously being homeless and on the streets you're always going to be up when things are happening in the city or town centre, it just makes sense. The only time I am crashed at this time is when I have taken too many prescription tablets and spice and it just whacks me out like a zombie. I am totally the opposite at the minute as Vinnie has been getting us loads of magic since the rock has gone. It's like I am always up and ready to go until about five a.m. but I am not arsed, anyway I like my life on the go not in one place for too long, nothing can catch up with you.

Kane has told us not to answer the phone to Vinnie and Ricky and let 'em know we have sold everything as they will probably want us to go back out with more while it is busy and he cannot be arsed tonight, he wants to have a bit of a buzz as we have money and drugs the only thing missing is a bird.

A couple of girls come in who are laughing and falling over each other they have pink cowboy hats on and scarf things around them saying Donna's Hen Night; they are a few years older than us and are quite a bit on the heavy side and showing of a lot of their cleavage. Kane notice the girls and shouts over to them.

"So who is Donna then, gals?"

"What's it to you likes?" the girl's reply in a thick Scottish accent.

"I wanted to buy her a McDonalds to be nice, Yo." Kane is smiling and has converted into his Gangsta image. He thinks this impresses the girls, but I always think he makes himself look like a nob head.

"She has gone back to the room pished, but you can buy us summat if ya want laddie."

"No worries, come here what do you want?" Kane pulls out the takings of the night from his pocket to try and impress, which it does to be fair, the girl's eyes light up like a Blackpool Illuminations in November.

The girls get their food; I cannot help noticing how quick they gulp down the two Big Mac meals with an extra chicken sandwich meal; not even coming up for air to answer to Kane's questions! Eventually they answer one: "What's your name gals?"

"I am Dorothy, this is Emma-Jo,"

"Well, pleased to meet you two princesses, this is Mo and George and I am Kane."

They are talking shit about where they are from and stuff. One of them keeps looking at me and smiling, but I want to get high on spice not fuck with a girl who can eat more than me and probably out wrestle me too? Kane is now giving me the eyes to support him in the quest as him and his girl are sharing chips, well she does not look too happy with this but the vibe is there for him to get some action from her. Fuck it, I think to myself, I might as well get involved.

"Dorothy whereabouts in Scotland are you from then?"

"Glesga," she tells me which I have to ask twice, I cannot really understand her they talk fast… but not as fast as they eat.

"I am going out for a ciggie; you want to join me, George?"

"Yeah, but I will have a joint instead."

"Nice, I will join you with the joint and you can walk us back to our B&B; it's only up the road."

As we leave McDonalds I hear Emma-Jo say to her pal, "We've drank, danced, eaten and now a smoke. Only one thing left to do to complete a good night, aye Dors?"

Mo tells us he is getting off back to the room. I share half the bag with him and tell him I will see him later on. He smiles at me and shakes his head as he takes another look at the girls walking down the pier. Dorothy is pulling her knickers out of her arse.

"See you later, George, be careful," the cheeky fucker laughs, but like always, I'm not arsed.

23

White Flash

Vinnie

I rang the lads earlier and all was well, but the fuckers are not answering now? It's just gone one thirty a.m. and the landlord of the pub has kicked us out. We had a good night in there and I think I may well be in with one of the birds behind the bar. Ricky has sold four bags to Simon and Michael who came in for a couple of pints. I bought them a couple of rounds and it pains me, but they are bringing in customers left right and centre. I actually think half of the staff on that pleasure beach is on my weed right now.

We leave the pub and walk down towards the B&B smoking a joint of skunk as I had ran out of spice. I remember telling Ricky about the girl behind the bar who I think I may be in with the next thing I remember is the WHITE FLASH and coming round with Ricky knocked out and beaten badly. I see two lads running up the road I cannot get a proper view of them because I am still spinning.

I begin to laugh for some weird reason when I look at Ricky, the poor fucker has broke both his hands, his toes and now has probably has some serious damage done to him. I am not sure if it is shock or I genuinely find it funny.

"Ricky, Ricky are you ok, pal?"

Mmuummhh. He mumbles some shit, which reassures me he is not dead. I feel the back of my head as it is hurting bad. There is blood on my hand. It looks like I have been hit with something from behind. I can feel the rage beginning to build inside me. I AM GOING TO DO SOME EVIL SHIT WHEN I FIND OUT WHO HAS DONE THIS! I kick Ricky and he comes round.

"What the fuck happened? Did you see who it was?"

"Yeah," he says in a low voice which sounds like his breathing is constricted. "It was fucking Dessie and his mate."

A sense of relief comes over me as I now know who I will be dishing my evil out to. I check my pockets, my money and weed has gone, even my cigs. The good news is that they left the safe key and they have not got my phone.

Ricky sits up and his face is already swelling up, his nose and mouth are bleeding and I think the black eyes are already swelling. This can be seen in the dark, so it must be bad. I mean, we have all had a kicking before, you have to ride the storm now and then and have a taste of life's true nature but always bounce back and I assure you I will be bouncing on heads very soon. I check myself over while he comes round proper and realise I have only had a crack on the back of my head and had my gear robbed.

"Have you still got your money and weed?" He does not answer so I check him. NO, it's gone, the money and over an ounce of weed.

A car goes past us and pulls up; it's the bird from behind the bar.

"Are you okay?"

"Not really, love. Can you take us to the hospital please?" I ask. I am gutted she has seen me like this as I thought I was on a winner with her, now I look like a loser and probably will have to get into her on the sympathy route. She jumps out of the cab and ask if I want her to call the police. "No love, no need for that, just a lift to the hospital would be fine."

We arrive at Blackpool Victoria Hospital and it is fucking rammed with idiots looking in the same state as Ricky. I thank Claire and tell her we will be fine and she should get herself home. I ring Kane and George and their phones are off. I ring Mo who is at the B&B.

"MO, WHERE THE FUCK ARE THEM TWO PRICKS!"

"They have copped off with two Scottish birds, mate. What's up?"

"Come down to the hospital with some spice, straight away we have been jumped by Dessie and his mate and have had our gear nicked off us. Get a taxi and hurry up. We are in pain, pal."

24

Should I Stay or Should I Go

Mo

The safe is in front of me. George and Kane are away till the morning and Vinnie and Ricky are in the hospital… and the safe with a kilo of weed and £5,000 in cash is in front of me. The money I stole from my family plus my drug debt will cover all this. The shame will go away eventually and I can go back home to my family and get off this spice and stop living homeless and be like all the other kids.

I look at the safe for another couple of minutes. I need a screwdriver and a blunt object and the safe with its contents is mine. There are loads of videos on YouTube I have seen on opening a cheap hotel safes and I know this is my opportunity. I know that if I take off the crest badge from the front of the safe I can pick it along with a tiny Allen key or I can just smash the safe from its fixings and take it out of the B&B with me and open it with tools tomorrow when I am well away from here! THE SAFE IS IN FRONT OF ME, my life can change right here tonight and I can go home! I lie on the

bed and close my eyes to gather my thoughts before
choose my actions I ask myself one last time: can I ever
be like all the other kids that's all I really want in life?

25

Five Minutes and I Was Arrested

Janey

I have never been to prison before, everyone used to say that I would end up there once I went into care – "she will end up in nick her", "she is going to do something to someone and end up going to prison for a long time" – I have heard it all before. What I never thought is that I would go into prison for twelve weeks for stepping into Piccadilly Gardens. I was there for just five minutes!

My solicitor did nothing as usual and I had the same magistrate who sentenced me not one week before, I knew I was in trouble but I did not expect this. I was battered by a girl on my first morning in the shower, I did not even see it coming she just hit me from the side and before I knew it I was beaten and bleeding.

It's weird though, I am glad it has happened to me, as that minute on the shower floor was my point of no return! I swore that instant I am never going back to drugs, prostitution or alcohol. I wish I could add men to that sentence but I cannot see that. I will pick my relationships wisely in the future, but for now it is about me, Janey the child, the girl, the young adult.

There is some real good staff here at HMP STYAL. I am going to work with them to get my life back on track. Debbie said to me that I have a life expectancy of eighty years and if every year was a page in a book, I have just been through six bad pages of my life, the other seventy-four pages of life I can write myself with support being there, I just need to accept the support and start writing the pages of my own life. Lee has been to see me and my family have been this morning. I have told them that I am taking charge of my life in a positive way. There were no tears from my eyes when I told them but plenty from my family and I am sure I saw Lee's eyes well up but not me, I've shed enough tears.

The biggest shock I had was seeing women in here in a worse place than me, far, far deeper than me in drugs, alcohol and loss of mental health. There are so many other related traits I can see too. Many of us have had a child taken off us, or some of us have fell victim to a bastard of a man who has physically and mentally abused us and of course, the child care system; all I speak to is girls who was in care at some point in their life. Then there is SPICE; everyone in here is on it. We are like slaves to it. Some of the things I have seen in four days are enough to change my life, my world and my outlook.

I can actually say for the first time since my childhood. I am happy locked up in a cell with no freedom. I am happy.

26

Discharged

Vinnie

Ricky is well fucked. He has been given a bed and everything; they think his ribs, jaw, nose and ankle may be broken. I asked how he broke his ankle and apparently it can happen as they twist and fall when being knocked out. I am allowed to leave after sitting on a plastic chair for four hours I was called in and given a few stitches and they cleaned me up and bandaged my head. Mo has fucking switched his phone off and probably fell asleep, the fucker! Wait till I get back there. I call Kane and his phone rings this time.

"Where are you?" I shout down the phone to him.

"Safe yo we pulled a couple of gals innit. Two beautiful girls I swear mine looks like Khloe Kardashian."

"Never mind that shit, we was fucking jumped by Dessie and his mate from behind. I have had stitches in the back of my head and Ricky is well fucked in a hospital bed, he won't be out for a couple of days at least. Get a taxi and pick me up at the hospital straight away."

"What the fuck man, we will kill 'em YO!"

"Have you heard from Mo?" I ask.

"Nah man, George has you heard from Mo?" I hear George say he got a text about an hour ago saying he will see him soon bro!

"What the fuck does that mean?" I ask.

"George says MO's phone is off now?"

This concerns me for a minute, but I realise I have the key and he cannot get the safe without actually smashing the room up and walking out with the safe under his arm, because that's what I figured I would have to do if I wanted the dough and had no key. A panic comes over me and I tell them to get here quick. " The Victoria Hospital," I say before slamming the phone shut.

I go and see Ricky before the taxi comes.

"How are you, pal?"

"I'm rough, mate," he grumbles. "Can you get me some spice soon as for the pain? Pain killers are shit I need more than they will give me in here."

"What do you remember?" I ask him.

"I saw Dessie's mate hit you from behind with a bar or a bat, you dropped straight away. I tried to have it with that fucker but they was all over me. They even stabbed me twice in the arse, the fuckers. As soon as I get sorted I am getting that fucking gun and putting it in his fucking head and his big daft cunt of a mate."

"The gun is gone, pal," I tell him.

"It's not, I watched George stash it." What a sneaky fucker I think to myself.

280

"Just chill pal, we will be back in a few hours. I need to get my head down for a bit we will be back later them two are picking me up."

As I say, this the phone goes off. Kane tells me he is outside the A&E front door. I say my goodbyes and I am off.

Kane and George are quiet on the ride back. I don't want the taxi driver knowing anything, I also get him to drop us back a few streets away. Should I end up doing some cunt in in the next twenty-four hours that they cannot lead him back to us, which is quite likely as my head is starting to bang and the pain is causing me to rage inside. Even the voice inside me is telling me to go crazy this time!

"What happened, Vinnie? How much did they take?" George asks with a tone of concern in his voice.

"They took around £600 from us both and around four ounces, it was actually less cash and less weed, but I have to cover my loses and these two will be sharing the loss, believe me."

"I know where the fuckers hang out," says George, "we have seen them at the square with a load of pissheads."

"Who the fuck gave them the number?" I ask.

No one answers, but Kane says that they could have got it from anywhere we have sold to half of Blackpool in less than a week. "Every local and tourist has bought off us. It's like super strong skunk at two thirds of the price they are paying up here. Everyone is ringing us and the number is being passed left right and centre."

We walk into the South Shore View B&B and see Pickwick sorting the tables out for breakfast, he does not say good morning or even look at us like a standard B&B owner, he just nods his head upwards in acknowledgement that we are present. Kane calls him Prickwick under his breath which actually brings a smile to my face. We climb the stairs up to our room, feet sticking to the carpet. I open the door just wanting to collapse on my bed and crash into a deep sleep enhanced by strong painkillers and spice, and then we see him, Mo the young boy. I know straight away… His eyes are still open and the blade is close to where his right hand is flopped, the blood is everywhere.

"WHAT THE FUCK, MO! WHAT THE FUCK! WHAT THE FUCK!" I can feel myself turning into hysterics.

Kane grabs me around my waist. "It's okay, pal, it's okay, calm down Vin, calm down mate. He has gone, there is no pain for him he has gone." George is just staring at him motionless.

The next minute or so is a blur, Kane puts a blanket over him but does not move him or anything, it's clear he has been in this situation before or been around death. He is calm, strong and decisive. George builds a joint and Kane calls the ambulance. I open the safe and take out the Oakley bag.

"George, put this in your room, pal." He goes into his room, I instinctively follow him. Kane goes down to tell Pickwick what's happened; I don't go back in the room from that point just sit outside waiting for the ambulance and of course, the police.

27

Just Another Day
At The Office

Vinnie

The ambulance men arrive, followed by the police and
the fire brigade. The police ask us all questions about
where we have been where we have come from, how
long was we out. They are pretty much happy with the
information and I feel that once they have ticked their
boxes and had the nod off the ambulance men they are
pretty much happy to go. I mean really, they seem happy
to go; they leave me a card of a councillor and tell me
that a support worker will be coming round in a few
hours to help and assist us in any way with our
bereavement.

The police have all Mo's details, as I gave them his
name, date of birth etc. He was down as missing from
home at an address in Wythenshawe. A worker from the
home has been contacted and is making their way to the
Blackpool now. I think they will contact his family and I
don't want to be around when they get here.

We go downstairs into the breakfast room whilst
they take his body out into the ambulance. Pickwick's

cleaning team have arrived for work and I can see him instructing them that our room is priority, not that I will be staying another night in there. We go around the corner of the dining room as I see the ambulance man coming into view of the lobby. I just cannot face him being taken away into the van. As soon as the van pulls away I break down into tears, me the leader, the strong one. I did not cry this much when my dad died. George is still in shock and has said nothing; we walk out on to the front and light a joint up. I ask Kane simply for conversation's sake how he got on last night with the weed.

"All gone," he says. "Thirty-five bags, mate."

I total up £700 in my head straight away. I take the money from him and tell him I will put it in the bag later.

Pickwick comes out to speak to us.

"Hello boys, I am so sorry for your loss. Life is short and really should be enjoyed, I honestly don't know how you are feeling right now but I have felt the pain you are going through daily for a long time. I just want to let you know there is another room for you upstairs and you are welcome to stay here for another week, free of charge. I lost my own son at a similar age to your friend and the pain has never left me. There is not much I can really do for you but if you need me for anything just give me a shout."

I am speechless I try to thank him and he just smiles and walks back into the B&B.

"We have to tell Ricky," says Kane.

"I know but let's just get cleaned up and showered first."

284

"I want to go pal, I mean leave this and move on I cannot take it! Give me some money and I am off, pal. I don't need it."

"What do you mean?" I ask George.

"I mean just give me that £700 and I don't want anything else. I am off, going back to Manchester, back to the tents, the hostels wherever."

"You cannot just go, you horrible fucker."

"Look, I cannot take it. I have to go. I cannot stay here in this place, please just give me some money. I will lose it, mate if I stay here."

I take a long look at George and I think I finally have figured him out. He has to keep moving from his problems, he cannot face anything, he really is a hobo, real damaged goods; something has happened to him in his early life that has screwed him well over. I take out the money and give him £600, there is £640 in the pile and I look at Kane to say *I know this is short*. I hand him the money and say take care pal.

"See youse in Manchester or wherever," and with that he throws me the key to his room and is gone.

28

What About Me

Vinnie

I pick up some cigs and a couple of bags of spice from the head shop. I also buy some papers and sweets for Ricky. When we get out of the cab I can see him leaning against the shelter in the smoking area. He looks awful, but going off what Kane told me a while back it was the kicking he was due. Dessie is not the only person he bullied on them camps.

"How are you feeling, pal?"

"I am sore, pal, really fucking sore. Did you get me some spice and cigs?"

I hand him the bags with everything in. He takes it and goes straight for the spice, which I can understand really.

"Listen, pal, I have something to tell you, you may need to sit down."

"I carnt, my arse is still bad from the stabbing. The bastards are well getting it once I am better."

I can see Kane is starting to fill up his emotions are hitting home.

"Look, it's Mo, he has killed himself in the hotel last night, slashed his wrist we all found him when we got back to the room after leaving you." Vinnie then looks at the floor the shock is kicking in and he does not know what to say or do, a voice inside is blaming himself and he can also feel guilt creeping in.

"Fucking hell that is bad, really bad what the fuck's he done that for? The crazy fucker I always knew there was something wrong with him. Did you get any money out of his pockets?"

I lift my head up and stare at Ricky my decision is made as to what I am going to do, I reply, "No pal we did not."

"I am so sore man I cannot even tell ya, did you get me some strong pain killers?"

I am now raging inside, I cannot believe this horrible bastard has changed the subject, one of our only friends in the world has took his own life a kid who we all thought we was looking after, took under our wing has took his life and he has not even flinched! Or shown a bit of emotion and has just shrugged off like it is second to his problem. I cannot stay here with him.

"Look, pal we have got to get off, the police and support workers are coming to see us to ask a few more questions, I just wanted to make sure you was sorted."

"Okay, no problem. I will see youse later, listen I know it's bad about Mo, but we split four ways now."

I cannot believe this cunt! I don't even mention George and he has not even asked. "Oh yeah, of course," I say with a smile.

Both me and Kane turn our backs and walk off together without saying a word to each other. Kane is completely aware of this fucker and his disregard for any other person in this world. The shit he has done to Janey and I bet there are others before her too. My mind is made up. I flag a cab down and ask to go back to the South Shore Hotel.

In the room I open the safe taking out the money and the weed.

"There is just over 5K here, pal and a kilo of skunk weed." I split the weed in to two containers shoving two thirds toward Kane and handing over £500. I have £4,500 and around eleven ounces of skunk which if I knock out in ounces I can get just under £2000. in return.

"Okay, pal it's like this. You can take that weed, both phones and sell all that for a fantastic return in a week! Or you can split it with that selfish shady horrible fucker, it's up to you but this here is all mine and I am going now and never returning back to this life, it's over for me, this is my goodbye."

"Sweet, Yo. I understand, fuck him he has what he deserves right now. I think I might stay here a few days before getting off back home to Manchester; I will probably go to my mum's or something, what about you?"

I just shrug my shoulders, it's not his business this is goodbye and he knows it. I give him a hug and leave the room and go out to the front of the B&B.

I hail a taxi and tell him to take me to Manchester – my sister's in fact. The solicitors have informed us a few days ago that the council have offered a settlement for us both of £79000 which is nearly £40000 for me. That is a deposit on a flat, a fork lift truck training course, a car, a Sky TV deal with broadband, the *Game of Thrones* series on demand, a girlfriend with a job, phone contracts, season tickets to Man City, progression, enslavement, loss of freedom and being part of the system worrying about terrorists and hating the council for giving us smaller bins! I never thought that I would be part of this again, but now I am about to embrace it with open arms. I am gone.

12 months later

I am walking through Manchester centre, shopping with Jennie for baby stuff, it's a bit early as she is only four months, but we are excited and its part of the pregnancy I want to enjoy this time. I see a homeless beggar ahead of us rocking whilst sat on the floor with his hood up. As we approach him he says in a hoarse and weak voice "spare some change, please." I walk past and look down. It's Ricky! Skinny, weak and looks like the streets have got the best of him – I am sure he is on heroin. The funny thing is, he does not even look up at me as we walk past. I squeeze Jennie's hand and walk on.

"It's a shame for them," she says.

"It is," I tell her, "I wonder how they ever ended up there."